DUTY TO DEFEND

JILL ELIZABETH NELSON

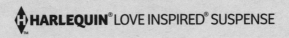

Recycling programs
for this product may
not exist in your area.

 LOVE INSPIRED BOOKS

ISBN-13: 978-1-335-54351-6

Duty to Defend

www.Harlequin.com

Printed in U.S.A.

The heavy rat-a-tat of automatic-weapon fire shredded the night.

Daci's heart pounded like a trip-hammer as she grabbed for the small pistol she'd strapped to her ankle for tonight's meeting, although what good the little peashooter might do against an automatic was anybody's guess.

Abruptly, the staccato burst of gunfire ceased, and Daci inched her head up above the hood of her car. With a screech of tires, the van raced away up the street.

Other gunfire blended with hers, and she searched for the shooter. There! Jax was rushing up the middle of the street, pistol raised and blasting, but the van didn't slow down as it disappeared into the night.

Jax broke off chasing the fleeing vehicle and raced toward the bullet-riddled VW, calling her name. Panic edged his tone.

Daci popped to her feet. "I'm here. I'm okay."

"No, you're not. You're bleeding." He gestured toward her arm.

She glanced down. Sure enough, warm blood trickled down her bare arm below the cap sleeve of her blouse. Now that the crisis was past, a hot burn in her biceps suddenly registered.

"Just a graze. Nothing serious."

"Nothing serious? Are you kidding? Someone tried to kill you."

Jill Elizabeth Nelson writes what she likes to read—faith-based tales of adventure seasoned with romance. Parts of the year find her and her husband on the international mission field. Other parts find them at home in rural Minnesota, surrounded by the woods and prairie and four grown children and young grandchildren. More about Jill and her books can be found at jillelizabethnelson.com or Facebook.com/jillelizabethnelson.author.

Books by Jill Elizabeth Nelson

Love Inspired Suspense

Evidence of Murder
Witness to Murder
Calculated Revenge
Legacy of Lies
Betrayal on the Border
Frame-Up
Shake Down
Rocky Mountain Sabotage
Duty to Defend

Visit the Author Profile page at Harlequin.com.

Blessed is he that considereth the poor:
the Lord will deliver him in time of trouble.
The Lord will preserve him, and keep him alive;
and he shall be blessed upon the earth: and thou
wilt not deliver him unto the will of his enemies.
—*Psalms* 41:1-2

To all the caregivers out there.
You know who you are!
Whether you care for aging parents,
developmentally challenged children or adults,
or a spouse or other loved one with
challenges that need special care,
you make the world a better place.

Acknowledgments

Bushel baskets of gratitude to my savvy editor
at Love Inspired Suspense, Elizabeth Mazer,
and to the rest of the editorial, copy and design staff
that work so diligently to make each book the best it
can be for our readers. Special blessings to my hubby,
who puts up with a lot of shushing when I'm nearing
manuscript deadline. Thanks so much for your patience,
sweetheart! And a special shout-out to you readers. Your
kind enthusiasm fuels my desire to write these stories.
Bless you and read on!

ONE

Stomach fluttering, Daci Marlowe paused outside her boss's closed office door and ventured a tiny smile. This was it—her first assignment as a US deputy marshal.

Finally!

After dealing with her siblings' toddler-then-teenage tantrums until her twenties had faded in the rearview mirror, she was more than ready to begin her own career. Not even the joker who had left the ribbon-bedecked basket with its smelly contents outside her duplex door this morning would cast a shadow on this moment.

Oh, yes, she *would* find out who the culprit was. That was a promise. The medium-size wicker basket had contained one jar of opened and spoiled baby food, a baby bottle a quarter full of curdled formula, an assortment of crumpled and dried baby wipes, and a diaper anointed with what her nose told her was vinegar. The block-lettered note read, "ENJOY YOUR NEW LIFE."

The personal nature of the practical joke should have narrowed her suspect list to one of her rowdy siblings, but something didn't quite fit, and she couldn't put her finger on what was off. But if she went with the theory, her brother Nate would top the list because he was the only one who lived within easy driving distance of Springfield, Massachusetts. However, he, as well as her other siblings, had called either last night or early this morning to wish her well on her first day on the new job, and her deeply ingrained imp-o-meter hadn't detected any pending mischief in their tones.

What if the culprit was none of them but, instead, an unseen watcher of her life? The question slithered like a snake down her spine. Daci suppressed a shiver. Stupid thought. No one but one of her brothers or sisters would link the trials and tribulations of an older sister raising a small herd of younger siblings with her first day of work in the Marshals Service.

She glanced down at herself for a quick ready-or-not inventory. Her shiny badge hung neatly from a lanyard around her neck. It lay face-out against her button-down shirt, while her government-issue firearm rested snug against her slacks-clad hip, its weight an underscore to the gravity of her new duties.

Today, I honor your memory, Grandma, by joining those who bring criminals to justice.

Inhaling a deep breath of law-enforcement office odors—scorched coffee, printer ink and stale pizza—she lifted her fist and rapped smartly on deputy commander Ross Reynolds's door.

"Come in!"

Her boss's gruff bark invited her into a square room just big enough to contain a large, well-used desk stacked with paperwork, a wheeled office chair in which he sat, a metal filing cabinet, and a pair of steel and plastic guest chairs. Daci suppressed a grin. Reynolds didn't like people getting comfortable sitting around. Yet, someone already occupied one of the guest chairs. She had expected to see the thick, jowly man seated behind the desk. The lanky blond in a navy suit and coordinating tie who assessed her with cool blue eyes had not featured in her visualization of this moment.

The stranger in the suit rose and stuck out his hand. "Jaxton Williams," he said. "Call me Jax."

She shook the man's long-fingered hand and murmured her name, following his lead by sticking to Daci, not the formal-sounding Candace. Jax's grip was firm and betrayed slight calluses. Despite his clothes, the guy wasn't a total pencil pusher, though not a member of the Marshals Service, either. What was he doing here?

Her gaze darted to Reynolds, who had folded his hands over his middle-aged paunch. The corners of his lips twitched as if he battled amusement. Was she interrupting another meeting? Hadn't she been told to report at 9:00 a.m. sharp? She resisted the impulse to check her watch.

"Shut the door and have a seat so we can get started," her boss said in that gravelly voice of his.

Fixing her eyes on him, Daci complied. The mystery man resumed his seat, also. Apparently, she'd get the answers to her questions soon enough.

Reynolds twiddled a pen between the thick fingers of his left hand, all humor erased. "You are aware of the situation with escaped felon Liggett Naylor."

"Of course, sir." Her heart leaped.

Surely, she wasn't being assigned to the fugitive recovery task force. Rookies didn't get high-profile cases. And this was as high profile as it got. Two deputy marshals were dead, for crying out loud, and the Marshals Service had a serious black eye for losing a major crime boss during transport from one detention facility to another.

But if she wasn't going to join the fugitive recovery task force, then why bring up Naylor at all? And what could this Jaxton Williams have to do with the case? She cast him a sidelong look. Faint swipes of gray highlighted the temples of his neatly trimmed blond hair, and crow's-feet lined the corners of his eyes. Around forty probably, less than a decade older than her age of thirty-two. Good-looking in an upper-crust sort of way. She'd had her fill of that type.

The stern set of his aquiline features and neatly squared shoulders screamed some sort of authority. A politician? Sure, that was it. The powers-that-be must be screaming for quick action against Naylor. But her deduction didn't answer the question of why she would be included in a political pacification meeting between a bigwig and her boss.

Reynolds pursed his lips. "It seems you have a particular skill set we need in this situation."

Daci's breath caught. What skill set had captured her boss's attention? Maybe he'd noticed the training record she'd set in Search and Seizure? Or the natural aptitude she'd demonstrated for interrogation? Few would suspect those skills were honed to a razor's edge *before* entering the training academy. A person didn't raise four younger siblings without morphing into a cross between professional detection dog and a finely calibrated lie detector.

"When Naylor went down for multiple counts of murder, racketeering and grand theft," Reynolds continued, "it's a little-known fact that his girlfriend, Serena Farnam, caved under interrogation and told us where to find him. We don't know if Naylor is aware of her role in his apprehension, but whether he knows or not, there is a slim chance he may be dumb enough to try to contact her—either to kill her in revenge or to reunite with her if he believes she's still loyal. We need you to stick to this woman like grease on a rag until Naylor is apprehended."

Dry mouthed, Daci stared at her boss. Multiple questions flew through her mind, but only one stuck to her tongue. "Why me?"

Reynolds looked away, focusing on some spot in the corner of the ceiling behind her head. Something about this situation had her boss a little reluctant—probably her inexperience. Daci sat up straighter. Whatever the mission, she'd do her best to exceed his expectations.

Jaxton Williams angled his body toward her.

"We think you stand a good chance of bonding with Serena at her new work site, maybe even becoming a trusted friend."

We? Daci gaped at him. Since when did a politician get consulted on Marshals Service assignments?

Her boss's gaze turned hard and sharp. "Because of his professional obligations to interact with Ms. Farnam—and his experience in the Marshals Service—Jax will be your backup in the woman's work environment. Somewhat in her home, as well...provided you succeed in getting invited into Ms. Farnam's social circle. We need you to make that happen."

Daci narrowed her eyes at the suit. "You're a marshal?"

"Former." A grin lifted one side of his chiseled lips. "This guy here—" he motioned toward DC Reynolds "—used to be my team partner, but I changed careers about five years ago and became a—"

"Kiddie lawyer," Reynolds burst out.

A wicked smile lit Jaxton's face, sparking his blue gaze and propelling Daci's silly heart into a backflip. "That's *Mr*. Kiddie Lawyer to you, Rey-Rey."

"Big talk from the guy who sits behind a partition in a warehouse reno where the phones never stop ringing and the voices never stop jabbering."

"I like my wide-open spaces. Beats your claustrophobic 'splendor' any day of the week." His gaze traveled the circumference of the small office. "And don't forget my private conference room in the back. It's furnished with a top-of-the-line folding table."

Reynolds snorted. "We can't all hit the big time."

The guys grinned at each other, and Daci heroically resisted the urge to roll her eyes. Her twin brothers, Nate and Noah, used to banter like this all the time at the dinner table, which was not a bad thing—usually. But the habit drove her nuts when she was trying to have a serious family discussion, and the discussion right now was about as serious as it got.

She still had no idea where this assignment was taking her—other than cozying up to a vicious felon's former girlfriend. It sounded like it would be an undercover operation—certainly an unusual choice for her first assignment. How would anyone come to the conclusion she had the skill set for this?

"What exactly is a kiddie lawyer?" Daci enunciated her question with the slightly too loud, slightly too cold precision that used to get the boys' attention at the meal table.

The smirks fell away, and both men fixed their stares on her. Daci raised her eyebrows. Apparently, the method worked with adults, as well. Who knew?

Jax offered a sober nod. "I work for a non-profit specializing in defending the rights and best interests of juveniles and/or mentally and emotionally handicapped adults who have entered the social services system. We're not *in* the system ourselves, so we can take *on* the system to address corruption or mismanagement if we need to do so. We follow our clients closely, even making regular visits to home or caregiver sites."

Warmth spread through Daci's insides. Score a big one for the suit for choosing such a difficult, yet worthwhile, career. Numerous crises embedded in her past could have used such an advocate. She smiled at the nonprofit lawyer, and he blinked back. Did his square jaw drop a few millimeters? What was up with that? Her frizzy strawberry blond locks, barely contained by a wrap net at the nape of her neck, and well-defined but ordinary features weren't exactly knock-'em-dead material.

Reynolds cleared his throat. "Jax has accepted a temporary assignment with the Marshals Service for this case."

"Very temporary and limited in scope." Jax's

intense gaze turned toward Daci's boss. "My primary focus will be the child—not Serena, not even Naylor. That's where our goals and interests intersect. If I have to choose between protecting the boy or apprehending Naylor, I will choose the child."

"Wouldn't have it any other way." Reynolds nodded.

Daci tapped a finger against her lower lip. "Am I correct in understanding that this child is Ms. Farnam's son?"

Honestly, it was like pulling teeth to find out what this case was all about. She'd learned during her orientation that Ross Reynolds was generally forceful and direct. Something about this situation had him tiptoeing like a ballerina on a crowded bus.

Her boss leaned his elbows on the scarred desk. "Yes, she has a little boy. A six-month-old infant that is assumed to also be Liggett Naylor's son—another reason there's an off chance he may try to contact her. You are assigned to shadow the mother under cover as her coworker. You and she will be starting work together on the same day, which should add additional opportunity for bonding.

"Because Serena has problems that have called into question her fitness as a mother, she has lost custody of him—at least temporarily. Jax has been assigned to the son as his legal representative, which gets him access to monitoring the child. He also observes the mother at her workplace for confirmation that she is rehabilitating and during set times when mother and son are reunited for supervised home visits. When you're around Serena, you and Jax are to behave as if you are strangers. But behind the scenes, the two of you will co-ordinate efforts on everything."

Daci shifted in her seat. What kind of pa-rental-fitness problems? "How much do the people at this workplace know about the dan-ger Serena Farnam may attract toward them? I mean, I don't want to speak out of turn and say too much on the job."

"The director, Naomi Minch, knows the whole picture," Jax answered. "I filled her in, and she agrees that Naylor would be a fool to approach his former girlfriend if he doesn't want to be recaptured. He's probably on his way out of the country as fast as he can go. However, she's on board with the two of us operating under cover to keep an eye on the situation, just in case."

"Right." Reynolds jerked a nod. "While Ser-ena is aware that her former boyfriend is in the wind, she laughed when police suggested he might seek her out. According to her, before he was arrested, Naylor was already losing interest in her. He's more than old enough to be her father and has a reputation for preying on vulnerable younger women, then discarding them. We offered protective custody or a protection detail, but she refused, so the arrangement we are discussing is Plan B. Serena has no idea we are planting undercover deputies. She needs to stay in the dark so she will trust you. Since her interaction with Jax has been somewhat adversarial, it will be important that she not realize you and he are working together. Now, go study the case file on your computer and get busy on this as of yesterday. Any further questions?"

"Lots," Daci said, "though I assume they will be answered in the case file. But, right now, I'd like to know why the baby is in the system."

Jax frowned and glanced toward his polished shoes. "Chase has fetal alcohol syndrome."

Daci went rigid. An image of her youngest brother Niall's FAS-distinctive features flashed across her mind's eye so clearly that it was as if it were only yesterday she'd so briefly held him close before he disappeared from her life.

"Sir," she said to Reynolds through gritted teeth, "from the detailed background check in my employment file you should know enough about my history to see this circumstance makes me the wrong person for this assignment."

Scowling, her boss slapped a palm on the desk. "Suck it up, Marlowe. You're a professional. Act like it."

Daci's hands balled into fists. "I'm *not* a professional actor, and I have no experience with undercover work. A job like bodyguard I could do in a detached manner regardless of the circumstances, but I have doubts about my ability to make this woman believe I want to be her friend."

Reynolds sat back, eyeing her grimly. "Then let me tell you the aspect of this case that makes you perfect for the assignment. Ms. Farnam has gotten herself on the straight and narrow and will start work tomorrow on a probationary basis at a day care. She's nervous and excited about her new career. You begin in the morning as her coworker—a very experienced and helpful coworker who can take her under your wing. Get the picture now?"

The bottom dropped out of Daci's hopes and dreams. This was her adult job. Finally! And her first assignment in her law-enforcement career was taking care of kids—just as she'd been doing for so many years. *Really, God?*

* * *

Jax's brows knit together. What had sucked the blood out of Daci's face?

This woman had already proved to be an intriguing enigma. She was respectful toward her boss without the usual eager-to-please rookie mannerisms. Perhaps entering the Marshals Service a decade older than the usual fresh-faced greenie contributed to her maturity and stability. It certainly seemed to make her more sure of herself than any rookie he'd met before. In fact, when it came to male banter, she'd decisively redirected the conversation. He'd almost burst out laughing at the irony of a rookie taking charge, but decided a sober face was the better part of wisdom. Certainly, the better part of professionalism.

He needed to make professionalism his plumb line in working with this intelligent, attractive deputy marshal, especially since she was precisely the sort of woman he would consider asking out…if she had any other career than law enforcement. The very nature of the job included extra danger and could get cops and their families killed. *Had* gotten his family killed. Bile scorched the back of his throat. He couldn't go there ever again.

"Get out of here, you two." Rey made a shooing motion with both hands. "Study that file together, then make like law officers and catch me a bad guy."

Daci rose slowly, blinking as if a bit dazed. "Is this really our best chance of nailing Liggett Naylor?"

"I hope not." The DC frowned, reaching for a folder on his desk. "We've got multiple teams working around the clock to track him down. If I had my way, we'd have this lowlife in custody before you showed up for kiddie duty tomorrow."

"We'll hope for that, then, sir." She turned on her heel and marched out.

Jax followed her into the bull pen of this branch office of the United States Marshals Service. Three other federal deputies and a clerical assistant/IT technician had computer desks placed at intervals throughout the space. Only the clerical desk was occupied, and the IT guy seemed mesmerized by his computer screen and didn't bother to acknowledge their entrance.

At the federal district courthouse yesterday, Jax had noted that the routine Marshals Service duties of providing protection and guard detail were being covered by other agencies. With all the stops pulled out to track down Liggett Naylor, the other deputies would be out scrambling after leads.

Grabbing a stray guest chair, Jax followed his new partner to a spot in the corner of the room near the printer. Everyone in the bull pen would have to walk behind her chair, sometimes bumping her desk, to get to their printouts. Newbs always got the worst desk placement. By the pinched look on Daci's face as she woke up her computer, this newb also thought she'd received the worst first assignment. Why? Given Rey's selection of her, she must have a history with kids. Maybe the problem was with the mother. She'd seemed very upset at the mention of FAS. Maybe he should finesse matters in that area.

He hunkered down beside her. "You'll no doubt discover a few things about Serena and Chase's social-services status when you bring up the file. Serena was thrown out of her home as a young teen and, unsurprisingly, got caught up in the street culture of drugs, alcohol and prostitution. Naylor was three decades older, but he took a fancy to her. Staying with him gave her a place to live and his money facilitated her...um, habits. When she showed up at the hospital drunk and in labor, and then Chase was born with fetal alcohol syndrome, he was immediately removed from her custody. Fortunately, that was a real wake-up call for her to get help for her alcoholism. The county put her in a three-month in-patient program, followed by three months at a halfway house, and now she's in intensive outpatient treatment."

"And the baby?" She arched a fine, dark brow.

"Chase will remain in foster care until his mother is nine months sober, and because of his special needs, the foster parents found a day care that offers therapy for challenged newborns. By arranging for Serena to work there, her job will teach her the skills to care for him and also provide daily supervised interaction between mother and son. She seems passionate about gaining the opportunity to raise him."

Sometime during his speech, Daci's stare had gone flat. She had the richest brown eyes he'd ever seen, unusual and a bit exotic with the light hair, but something about this conversation unearthed an ancient pain that lurked in their depths. "Why are you putting him at risk by letting her have him again? I thought you were the child's advocate, not the mother's."

"I am, which is why she didn't get Chase back as soon as she graduated from the halfway house." He offered a smile that wasn't returned. The old Williams charm must be experiencing an off day—or else an extra-challenging subject. "Ultimately, it's the judge's decision, but I fought hard to keep Chase in a guaranteed stable environment until the mother has a chance to get her feet under her in the real world. Thankfully, the judge saw the wisdom in that idea. On the other hand, I believe in giving families a chance to heal and reunite. Continued sobriety is possible."

Daci's upper lip curled. "But not probable, especially when the scrutiny comes off and the stakes of losing the kid goes away."

"You speak from experience, I take it?"

Rather than answering, she turned back toward her computer screen, revealing a fine-boned profile enhanced by a delicately upturned nose and a firm, rounded chin. If she'd tried to charm *him* with a smile, he had no doubt it would have worked. Just as well for him that she hadn't tried.

"Can you see well enough to read along with me?"

The tone of her question left no doubt that she wouldn't allow him to direct the conversation back to his question about her past experience. Let no one say he couldn't take a hint, but the legal bloodhound in him was on the hunt. Would it be out of line for him to request her file from Rey? Probably. He'd have to satisfy his curiosity the lawman-turned-lawyer way—

evidence collection and finessing information from witnesses.

Marlowe wasn't a terribly unusual surname, but it did ring a bell from some type of years-ago media hoopla about tragedy and scandal in a filthy rich founding father–type family from Boston. Surely, this down-to-earth Marlowe wouldn't turn out to be from that bunch, but he wouldn't rest easy until he'd tracked down the reason for his hazy recollection. Online homework for tonight.

Two hours later, he and Daci had exhausted the information in the files on Serena Farnam and Liggett Naylor, uncovering and discussing some extremely disturbing facts about the latter. A career criminal from a single-parent household—father unknown—he'd been involved in everything from home burglaries and drug dealing to bank holdups and freight-cargo heists, most of these involving the murder of any possible witnesses.

By the time law enforcement brought him down, he was a kingpin in various criminal enterprises ranging from stolen-vehicle chop shops to hot-property fencing rings and rack-eteering. Anyone who got in his way was annihilated. *Homicidal maniac* would be a mild description of the charismatic and remorseless criminal with a trail of dead bodies and destroyed lives in his wake.

"How does society breed these animals?" Jax shook his head.

"You're blaming society as a psycho-mill now?" She gazed at him coolly.

He almost responded with a quick defense of his comment, then noted the slight curve at the corners of her mouth. She was teasing him—and a goofy heart-thump startled him into openmouthed silence.

Her grin broadened. "With your years in the Marshals Service, I'd think you would have run into plenty of this type along the way. What soured you into litigator over lawman?"

"Soured?" The sudden taste on his tongue matched the word.

The churning in his gut was a toxic cocktail of grief, guilt and regret. A timely reminder of why he could not allow himself to respond to his attraction to this woman.

He sat back in his chair and looked away from those deep brown eyes. "It was either get out of law enforcement or have my own humanity eroded into oblivion. God opened the door for me to do something that daily allows me a different way to protect the most innocent from the most depraved."

"God opened the door, or did you make a

choice that required drastic action?" Again, that fine eyebrow went up, but then she waved a dismissive hand. "Never mind. I guess I used to have more of that faith stuff than I do now. Bottom line, I admire you for admitting when you needed a change and then making it happen."

Jax bit back further remarks on faith. Who was he to talk when he sometimes wrestled with his own?

He leaned closer to Daci. "My bottom line? If this guy does try to reenter Serena's life, we need to nab him before he can inflict any damage—either by hurting Serena or grabbing his son. Serena and Chase are so close to becoming a healthy family."

Her mouth tightened. "If that's going to happen, she needs to do more than stay alive and off the sauce. She's going to have to perform an extreme makeover on her taste in men. That's rare. I rate their chances a long shot, but I'm all for offering them the full protection of the law."

A low rumble originating from her belly punctuated her last sentence, and a blush crept up her neck.

"Hungry?" Jax grinned.

She managed an answering smile and rubbed

her middle. "Time got away from us, and my tummy noticed."

Jax rose. "I know a place a few blocks away that serves the best clam chowder in a fresh-baked bread bowl I've ever tasted."

"Sam's Clams?"

"You've eaten there?"

"The day I came in for orientation. My new coworkers recommended it. Apparently, the charm of the place is an open secret around here."

"I remember that from my marshal days." His grin faded.

Why was he inviting Daci Marlowe to have lunch with him? It would have been just as easy to wave and walk out to each seek their own meals.

"Okay, partner, you talked me into it." Her lighthearted words jerked him back into the moment. "A working lunch it is."

A tight coil unwound in Jax's belly. A working lunch. That's all this was. He could do that.

They left the office and walked out the building's glass doors into the warmth of a New England spring day. The sky was blue and nearly cloudless, and a breeze carried the scents of flowering landscape bushes.

Crossing the small courtyard to the side-walk, Jax stuffed his hands into his pockets and fell into step with his companion. "Have you always lived in Springfield?"

"Moved here from Boston when I got the posting. This is my first duty day."

"That's why you didn't eat breakfast this morning."

She sent him a sharp look as they entered the crosswalk of a busy street, along with a straggling line of pedestrians. "How do you know I didn't?"

He smirked. "First day. First assignment. Oh, yeah, I remember what that was like. Hunger was gnawing a hole in my stomach by noon, but if I had eaten breakfast before I reported for duty, I would have puked on my boss's shoes."

A full-throated laugh burst from Daci, and Jax's heart tripped over itself at the husky, happy sound.

The roar of an engine and screech of tires yanked his head around. A small SUV jetted around the corner through a red light and roared straight at them.

TWO

Icy-hot sparks shot through Daci's middle as she and Jax leaped forward. The SUV whipped past them so close the air current shoved her into a silver-haired woman ahead of her. With a shriek that blended with the startled cries of others in the crosswalk, the woman sprawled to the pavement. Heaving in long breaths, Daci squatted beside her. The silver-haired woman lay on her side, her complexion bleached, her eyes and mouth as round as eggs.

"Are you alright?"

The woman blinked up at Daci. "That car nearly ran you over. What is *wrong* with people today?"

Daci shook her head. "I can't answer that, ma'am. Are you able to stand?"

"I—I don't know." She rubbed her elbow and attempted to sit up but subsided with a groan. "My arm hurts…and my hip."

"Stay still." Daci put a hand on the woman's shoulder. "We'll get paramedics here."

"I'll call for an ambulance," a deep voice said from behind her.

Daci looked up to find Jax gazing down at them. A strange buoyancy filled her chest at seeing him standing there, safe and sound, tapping on his phone to call for assistance. She glanced around to see if anyone else had been hurt. People milled in the street in various stages of wide-eyed shock. On the sidewalk, a few gawkers excitedly chattered on their cell phones. Traffic was at a standstill, though a few impatient souls were starting to honk.

Sirens began to wail in the distance as DC Reynolds and the desk clerk, Randy Lathrop, hurried out to them in the street. Daci remained beside the injured woman as her co-workers took charge and rerouted traffic until the local authorities could arrive and assume command.

Daci rose as her boss strode up to her.

"Glad to see you're okay," he said.

"Just a little shaken, sir."

"See what you can do to get witnesses to stick around until they can be interviewed. Folks are trying to slip off and get on with their day."

"Will do, but if nothing else, the traffic cam might give us a lead on the perp."

Reynolds grimaced. "If it was working. Road construction in the vicinity has been interrupting coverage. I know because Randy has been running automated searches of footage for any of Naylor's known vehicles suddenly appearing on the road."

Soon, law enforcement and emergency personnel had cleared the scene, and Jax and Daci stood together near a squad car giving their statements to Detective Herriman, who was in charge of the investigation. By the familiarity of the greeting between the two men, Herriman apparently knew Jax either from his deputy marshal days or from his current gig as a lawyer.

"I doubt I can contribute much to the information pool." Jax scrubbed his fingertips through the hair above one ear. "It was a bright red compact SUV. I have no clear recollection about the license plate, except that it was Massachusetts. Make and model escaped me as I scrambled out of the way."

"Understandable." Herriman made notes on his electronic tablet. "At least your account tallies with the majority of witnesses. A few descriptions we got ranged from monster truck to souped-up sports car."

Jax chuckled. "If only the general public had a clue about the unreliability of eye-witness accounts. But I guess I can't claim superiority in that area."

The detective grinned as he turned toward Daci. "Do you have anything to add, ma'am?"

"Daci Marlowe, new with the Marshals Service." She stuck out her hand, and Herriman shook it. "I may have a little to contribute. The vehicle was a late-model Toyota RAV4. Definitely Massachusetts license plate. I only remember two digits and a letter. Not necessarily in this order—three, eight and E. The driver was a male Caucasian, mid-to-late thirties. I didn't see anyone else in the vehicle, and in the blur of leaping out of the way, I didn't catch any facial details."

Jax and Herriman stared at her like she'd grown a second head.

She stifled a smile. "You might want to write that down."

"Uh, yes, absolutely." The detective pecked at his tablet.

A short time later, she and Jax were cleared to leave the scene, and they headed up the block toward the restaurant.

"Do you have any idea how unusual that was?" Jax leaned his head down and spoke close to her ear.

The sensation of his breath against her cheek was pleasant, but she made herself ignore it and put a few extra inches of distance between them.

"I agree," she said, keeping her voice neutral and professional. "Absolutely nuts if he was attempting a hit-and-run in the middle of the day on a busy street. I suppose the perp might have been substance-impaired, but if not, he sure couldn't claim distracted driving as cause for running a red light. He had to turn a corner. That smacks of deliberation. But why us? Or were we random targets?"

"Good questions, but no, I meant the details you remembered from a split-second, crisis experience. That's not normal."

Daci stopped and faced him. He must be about six feet three inches to her five feet seven inches, which meant she looked up a significant distance to meet his gaze. Those blue eyes were clear and cloudless. Hers? Well, he was probably glimpsing the fringes of the storm that brooded inside her.

"You're right. I'm not normal." If she couldn't manage utter calm, at least the tone emerged quiet and fiercely controlled. "With the way my life has gone since my earliest memory, I've had to develop certain skills so that my loved ones and I could survive. I don't have a clue what it means to live in *normal*. I wish I did. So many times, I've prayed to God, begging for normal to somehow find me. It never has." She broke eye contact. "Thanks for the lunch offer, but I've changed my mind. If you'll excuse me, I don't think I can eat anything. I'd better get back to my desk. See you tomorrow at the day care."

She chewed out those last two words as she hurried away. If this first day of the rest of her life diverged any more radically from all she had confidently expected, she might simply implode into a splat on the sidewalk.

An hour later, she sat at her desk, staring at her computer screen, a half-eaten candy bar and a mug of cold coffee at her elbow. That incident in the street today puzzled her. Had the driver been impaired by drugs or alcohol to the point where he had been unaware of pedestrians? But his driving had seemed anything but erratic as he shot toward Jax and her like an arrow off a bowstring.

She'd tried running through the system the scrap of license-plate identification she'd remembered. However, following up on the number of RAV4s that popped up was beyond her ability, even factoring in the color of the vehicle. Red was highly popular. If she wanted to identify the driver, she'd have to approach this from a different angle. She came back to the same question: Who had been the driver's target?

Jax may have made enemies during his days in the Marshals Service, maybe even more enemies during his dealings with volatile family court situations. Or could the target be her? She wanted to believe that the idea was ridiculous. Unless the attempted hit-and-run was connected to that stupid prank with the basket of rotten baby paraphernalia. What if the disgusting housewarming gift was not a brotherly prank, but a taunt with evil intent? The advice in the note to "enjoy" her life suddenly took on sinister overtones.

No use indulging needless paranoia. Chomping a bite out of her candy bar, she picked up her cell phone from the desk. A quick text to Nate, thanking him for his "thoughtfulness," would settle the matter one way or another. He'd either acknowledge his twisted gift or have no idea what she was talking about. If she scored zero with Nate, she'd check with her other siblings. One of them *had* to be the culprit. The alternative was too creepy, if not downright scary.

Daci shot off a tongue-in-cheek thank-you, then turned her attention back to the research she was conducting on therapy for fetal alcohol syndrome babies. Virtually raising her siblings almost from her earliest memory had prepared her well for normal day care duties. Her boss was right about her mad skills in that area, but she'd never cared for a FAS infant.

That opportunity, which many would have considered a burden, had been denied her. Daci's parents claimed her newborn baby brother Niall died at the hospital, but with no funeral being held for him, she'd never fully had closure. Where was he buried? Her parents wouldn't tell, and to this day, she didn't know and likely never would. As yet, she hadn't found a way to make peace with that blank spot in her history.

At least tomorrow she'd have an opportunity to make peace with Jax for her abrupt abandonment of their lunch plans. He hadn't meant anything insulting in his remark that she wasn't normal, but the whole overload of the day had gotten to her in that moment.

She'd have to step up her game if she didn't want him to write her off as a flake, which would be so unfair, since she'd never flaked on anything in her life. This case was extremely important on a society-impacting scale, even though parts of the assignment were a disappointment to her personally. Like Reynolds had told her: *Suck it up, Marlowe.*

While they were studying the files on Farnam and Naylor this morning, Jax had explained that he visited the day care frequently because many of the children were his clients. When he walked in tomorrow, she'd be ready for him with a friendly smile and, if they had a private moment, an apology.

By the time her shift ended, Daci was more than ready to leave the office. But even though she was done with her work for the day, another matter needed to be resolved before she could really relax. She had some thinking and research to do on her basket mystery.

During the drive to her apartment, her tired brain sorted through the results so far. Nate, who was swamped with starting a dentistry practice in Worcester, Massachusetts, and planning a wedding with his fiancé, had responded to her "thank you" text with a question mark and puzzlement emoji. She received a similar response during her afternoon break when she texted Noah, who was on a journalism assignment in London. She could cross them both off her list. If either brother had been behind the prank in person or by arrangement, he would have been proud to take credit and laugh at her scolding.

She pulled into the carport of a large Victorian home converted to side-by-side apartments in the quiet Pine Point neighborhood. A chorus of greetings from the porch of the Victorian house next door met her ears as she exited her little VW. Daci waved at three mixed-age women, members of a group home for mentally challenged adults, who resided there.

She'd been intrigued by the place when she'd moved in a week ago, and had gone over to meet the residents. In addition to rotating shifts of house mothers, there were six residents—two with Down syndrome, two with autism, one with fragile X syndrome and one with FASD. Their intellectual capacities varied from gifted in areas to slow across the board, but poor emotional and social skills guaranteed their need for a supervised environment for the rest of their lives. Once her life settled down a little, she might find time to go over and volunteer, but not today.

"Have a good evening," she called to her welcoming committee and trod up the three steps onto the porch. At least there were no more weird gifts awaiting her.

Inside, she changed into comfy jeans and T-shirt, then picked up her phone to call her sisters, Amalie and Ava. She was about to peck the speed-dial button for Amalie when her screen lit up and her ringtone began. Am had beaten her to the call. Most likely Ava was present, too, since they shared an apartment near Dartmouth University in Hanover, New Hampshire. Only two years apart in age, the sisters enjoyed a close relationship, despite or maybe because of their differing personalities. Amalie, the elder, was on the serious side, introverted and cautious, while Ava was bubbly and outgoing.

Daci answered and greeted her sister.

"How was your day, Mamasis?" Amalie lilted.

Warmth filled Daci at the familiar, affectionate nickname—though her sibs had sometimes changed it to "Nemesis" if they were at odds with her over some sort of growing pains.

"I'm here, too," Ava chimed in.

"Can't tell you the details," Daci answered, "but I've been assigned a small role in a high-profile case."

Feminine squeals blended.

"Awesome," Ava said.

"Does it involve danger?" Amalie's tone went cautious.

"No more than any law-enforcement assignment. Risk is part of the job."

Ava chuckled. "Our mamasis, the adventurer. I suppose you couldn't bear any sort of mundane career after the supreme challenge of raising us."

They all laughed.

"Which of you sent me the 'welcome to your new life' basket I found outside my door this morning?"

For a beat, stone silence answered.

"Must have been the neighborhood welcoming committee," Amalie said.

"Yeah, neither of us thought of doing anything *that* nice. Wish we had."

"What was in it?" Amalie was ever practical.

"Small stuff. Pretty much useless for my current lifestyle." If her sisters weren't in on the joke, no way was she going to freak them out by detailing the basket's contents.

"Wasn't there a card?" Am asked.

"Nothing that identified the sender."

"Weird," Ava said.

The conversation veered off into other topics, like Amalie's upcoming graduation with a major in archeology, followed by a summer internship at an ancient civilization site in New Mexico. Ava lamented the impending absence of her sister as she stayed behind at school, slaving toward her undergrad degree in Film and Media Studies. Daci alternately congratulated and commiserated. Twenty minutes passed quickly, and they ended the call.

If the gift basket was not an off-the-wall inside joke from her often-wacky nearest and dearest, then who had left it for her and why? In light of the seriousness of the attempted hit-and-run, should she report the incident to her boss? To the local police? Unfortunately, she no longer possessed the physical evidence that might yield forensic clues. She'd chucked the gross object into a Dumpster at the nearest gas station.

That night, such dilemmas, as well as flashbacks of the SUV bearing down on her and Jax, invaded her dreams. Her alarm clock's blare rolled her out of bed, groaning and mumbling under her breath. It was a harsher joke than spoiled baby food that she had to dress civilian casual and leave her badge in her dresser drawer on just her second day of work.

Her sidearm she put into a cloth bag to be taken into the day care director's office and kept under lock and key. Not the best scenario if Liggett Naylor showed up, because she'd have to run to retrieve it. There had been a brief discussion with DC Reynolds about her wearing a small pistol strapped to her ankle, but they'd discarded the notion. Packing a gun while she cared for small children was unacceptable.

Well before the seven o'clock opening time, Daci approached a squat brick building with a sign over the door that read Little Blessings Day Care. Judging by the name, this was a faith-based care center. Unusual choice for placement of a ward of the government, but Jax had said that, while not all pint-size clients here had special needs, this day care offered programs for those who did. Perhaps Chase's mental and physical challenges were the deciding factor in placing him in this one.

Daci paused inside the front door. The interior was brightly lit, revealing a foyer with a currently unmanned check-in desk standing outside a wall of glass that separated the foyer from a large open play area. Child-sized tables dotted a carpeted interior that featured separate sections for reading, crafts, toys and games. Doorways at the far end of the large room were labeled by age group.

A few adult workers moved around the play area. Children wouldn't start arriving for another twenty minutes. Daci had thought the environment would assail her with desperation to escape back into the adult world. Instead, the scents of wet wipes, spilled juice and small-child sweat drew a deep calm from her core. There was something to be said for familiarity. And nostalgia. It hadn't always been easy caring for her siblings, but she had some great memories of them from when they were this small.

A door to her left opened, and a petite, middle-aged woman with graying hair emerged, several file folders in the crook of one arm. According to the label on the door, this person was the director.

"You must be Daci Marlowe," the woman said, stretching out her free hand. "I'm Naomi Minch, and my staff graciously allows me to believe I run this joyful madhouse."

Daci smiled as she shook the director's hand. She was well on her way to liking her temporary boss. This day was actually getting off to a good start.

"Here," she said, and handed Naomi the sack holding her gun. "You know where to put this. I'll collect it after hours."

The director grimaced and accepted the bag gingerly. She hustled into her office and returned in a few moments, minus the bag.

A whoosh and rush of fresh air behind Daci announced someone coming in the front door. Jax? A little early for legal aid to arrive, but… Daci turned to face the newcomer, and her welcoming smile faded into openmouthed amazement. Dismay might be a better term.

Somebody please tell her this person was not her assignment.

The garishly made-up woman's anxious gaze darted from Naomi to Daci and back again. "I'm on time somewhere for once, aren't I?"

"Of course, Serena," Naomi answered kindly.

The woman wriggled her whole curvy body like a puppy who'd been praised. "Wow! Cool!"

Naomi stepped forward. "I'd like you to meet another new employee. Serena, this is Daci. Daci, this is Serena. You'll both be working with our infants."

"Hi." Serena's purple-painted lips curved into a smile, and she waggled a set of fingers at Daci.

The sharply filed nails were painted a brilliant shade of magenta sprinkled with glittery spangles. Those would have to go. As Daci lifted a hand in return greeting, she resisted glancing at her own neatly trimmed fingernails.

Surely, it wouldn't be her responsibility to instruct the young woman in grooming details, as well as the nitty-gritty of childcare. The task would challenge a professional makeover expert. Short, stiffly spiked hair sported streaks of hot pink between puffs of artificial yellow, sticking out like sheaves of wheat straw. Distressed jeans and the multicolored blouse that hung off one shoulder screamed wannabe teenager rather than twenty-three-year-old mother.

Daci stifled a deep groan. Classic! Addiction stunted the natural maturing process. She understood that concept better than most people on the planet, but bitter experience had left her cold toward the addict caught up in the phenomenon.

"Come on, ladies." Naomi motioned them deeper into the building. "Let me show you the infant rooms, and I'll introduce you to the lead teacher for that age group. Then we can issue your staff polo shirts we want you to wear every day at work."

Daci resisted the urge to wipe imaginary sweat from her brow. One fashion change would be taken care of without her having to add it to her already brimming plateful. She followed the day care director, dragging heavy chains of doubt about her ability to pull off the assignment of chumming with a recovering addict.

Jax leaned a shoulder against the doorjamb and watched Daci interact with a one-year-old on the nursery floor. Since her back was to him, and she was engaged with the little girl, Daci hadn't noticed his entrance. Her inattention to him suited Jax fine—it gave him an opportunity to observe this fascinating woman when she had no reason to be self-conscious.

He'd spent longer than he'd be willing to confess researching her online last night. He gave himself the excuse that he needed a solid sense of the background and experiences of his colleague, which was only part of the reason for his interest—maybe the smaller part. His discoveries had astonished him. Daci, more than most, had a web presence that had nothing to do with social media. In fact, as far as he could tell, she didn't participate in social media at all, and he didn't blame her. The professional media had already hurt her enough.

Their documented history of Candace "Daci" Marlowe gave fresh meaning to the term "poor little rich girl." Not that anybody looking at her understated grooming and attire would ever guess that her personal resources could put her in with the jet set rather than the workaday world. No doubt, her parents' antics had soured her on empty glitz and glamour, but she could have easily chosen a quiet life, out of the spotlight, without putting herself in danger. Why choose a career in law enforcement? Had witnessing her grandmother's murder left her with a score to settle with the bad guys of the world?

As much as he'd discovered in his research, Jax still had a lot of questions about Ms. Marlowe. It was anyone's guess whether she'd offer him any answers, and he had reasons of his own for not pressing for that level of intimacy, despite his attraction to her. He'd have to force himself to rein in his need-to-know mind. Easier said than done.

"Ja-ax!" Serena's singsong voice made two syllables of his name.

He turned to find the young woman scurrying up to him, bright red lips pulled wide in a grin. Jax stiffened, then ordered himself to relax.

Last time Serena had rushed toward him like that had been in court when he'd successfully argued not to allow Chase to be placed with her until she'd proved herself capable of remaining sober. She hadn't been happy with him in that moment and had used vivid language to clue him in on her feelings. At least it had only been words. He'd thought she was going to use those nails on his face.

"Hello, Serena," he said as she invaded his personal space.

Despite her tendency to overpaint herself, she was a pretty woman, and with sobriety, the health of her personal appearance had steadily improved—eyes clear not bloodshot, cheeks filled out rather than gaunt, and interesting hair clean rather than lank with grease and neglect. "You're looking well today."

She wriggled at the compliment. "I feel good, and I'm doing real good. Everything's perfect, except..." The smile abruptly fell away, and a pout took its place.

"Except what?" Jax rose to the bait.

"Chase isn't here today." Daci supplied the answer as she came to stand with them.

His breathing hitched. "Where is he?"

"Those foster parents of his called him in sick," Serena said. "I think they're making up excuses. Like, how am I supposed to bond with my son and learn how to care for him if they keep him away from me?"

"You don't trust people much, do you?"

"Why should I?" Serena crossed her arms over her chest. "All my life, people have done nothing but mess with me."

A troubled expression flitted across Daci's face, and she laid a hand on the shorter woman's shoulder. "I get that sentiment totally, but it really is against the rules to bring a sick child to day care."

"Ja-ax." Serena gazed into his eyes and smoothed the lapels of his suit jacket with her palms. "Would you please check on my baby for me?"

He took a half step backward. "I can do that."

Poor Serena. Her life experiences so full of certain types of men had her thinking that any request made to a man had to be based on sex appeal in order to get his agreement. No doubt, her counselors were working with her in this area, but it took a while to overcome deeply ingrained mind-sets.

"Oh, thank you!" Serena folded her hands together. "Like, as long as I tell myself his foster parents are making stuff up, I can be mad, but if my little boy really is sick, then I'm going to be sad. I need to know. You know?"

"I think Mr....er, Jax gets it," Daci said, sticking out her hand toward him. "Daci Marlowe, teacher's assistant."

Jax didn't miss a beat in shaking her hand. If Daci were to have a chance at gaining Serena's trust, it was important the young mother not be aware that Daci and he were previously acquainted. Serena Farnam had a highly developed sense of paranoia that would wreak instant havoc if she thought people were conspiring behind her back, even if it was for her own good.

"Jaxton Williams, juvenile rights attorney."

"You must represent young Chase," Daci said. "Serena's been telling me about her situation." She sent a kind smile toward the younger woman. "It's got to be tough."

Serena's intense expression lightened. "Yeaaaah." She breathed out long and low, as if such simple understanding meant the world to her.

An infant in a nearby crib began fussing, and Serena turned toward the sound. "I'll get him. These babies are so cu-u-ute!" She practically skipped away.

Daci's gaze followed the younger woman, a small frown on her lips. Jax cleared his throat, and she met his look.

"Since Chase isn't here, I'd like to see little Annie Brown and speak to her caregiver."

Daci smiled. "That would be me today. Follow me to the changing room, and I'll talk with you while I change her diaper. She crawled past me a few minutes ago, while I was finishing up with another child, and I thought she smelled a bit ripe."

At Jax's low groan, her smile morphed into a smirk as she scooped Annie up.

"Do you provide nose plugs?" Jax followed her toward a side room.

"Wimp," she said under her breath.

"I heard that."

Daci's answering chuckle warmed Jax from the ground up. She laid the child on the changing table and tickled the little girl's plump belly. Annie giggled and kicked.

"Hold still, sweet stuff." Daci began the changing process.

Jax stood rooted, staring, his heart shredding into tiny pieces. He'd visited this day care before, watched other babies being changed—though maybe not from this close up—but this moment was starkly different. Daci didn't look a thing like Regan, and if their daughter had been born, she would have been much older than Annie, almost ready for kindergarten, but something about the way Daci moved, the expression on her face, the tone of her voice as she spoke to the little one hit him like brass knuckles with fresh realization of what he had lost. A deep groan wrenched his gut.

Daci's head turned sharply. "Are you all right, Jax? You look like the Red Cross took the last pint of your blood."

He blinked down hard against the wet sting behind his eyes. "Yeah, I'm fine. Or I will be." He opened his eyes to find her holding the little girl, who had gone limp and was sucking her thumb.

"Did you really have some questions about Annie, or did you need an excuse to talk to me?"

"Both." *Get a grip, Williams.* "When you changed her, did you notice any bruises?"

"No, just healthy baby bottom."

"Good." Jax smiled. "That's what I expected to hear. Annie had a rough start in a toxic environment, but the dad has custody now, and she's been thriving. This was basically a final follow-up visit."

"Aren't these kinds of visits more social services territory?"

"Sure, but that department is spread so thin they're more than happy to enlist the help of a nonprofit like ours to pick up the slack. I'll write up my report, and they'll put it in their file. At the next court date, Annie will likely be released from the system into the mainstream. We call that a success story."

"Glad to hear it."

Daci held the child toward him, and he received the warm bundle. The girl stared at him for a few blinks, then laid her head on his shoulder and closed her eyes.

"She likes you and trusts you."

"I like her, too." He gazed down at the head of wispy brown hair.

"You're a natural. Any little Williamses at home?"

"No, not married anymore." Jax grimaced. "That's a story for another time. I need to get going and stop at Chase's foster home. How are you doing with Serena?"

"You saw." Daci rippled her shoulders. "She may be sober, but she's still a hot mess. I've stuck close to her all day and have begun to believe she genuinely wants to be a good mother to her son, but she's so pathetically clueless about what that entails."

"Contrary to her airhead demeanor, which I suspect is an ingrained facade to make her seem no threat to the predators in her environment, testing has shown she's bright. She's also motivated. She'll learn. No sign of our target?"

"Nary a one. Though I don't suppose he's going to announce his presence beforehand."

"He might call or text Serena."

"Workers here can't use cell phones except on break. Following her to the break room when I'm supposed to be on duty would be irresponsible in regard to the children, and it would look suspicious to Serena, but I've kept close watch to see if she exhibits any nervousness when she comes back on duty. I don't think she'd be able to hide her reaction if he reached out to her. Even if she believes he doesn't know she betrayed him, anyone would get the willies if contacted by an escaped felon. Besides, the Marshals Service is monitoring her cell communications."

"Do you have a plan to get into her circle of friends?"

Daci's expression clouded. "I'm going to express interest in attending an addiction-recovery meeting. If she accepts me as one who understands her issues, I should be a shoo-in."

"Sounds like a great plan to me, but you don't look happy about it."

"This is a world I thought I escaped. I'm not eager to revisit it."

"Understood. Hopefully, Naylor will be in custody again soon, and you can move on to a new assignment."

"One more thing, I want to apologize for leaving you abruptly yesterday. I'm not usually so touchy."

"No problem. It was an unsettling day."

Daci smiled up at him. "I appreciate your patience."

He made himself turn away before he blurted out an invitation to revisit their canceled meal plan. Dating Daci was out of the question.

A few minutes later, little Annie had been tucked into a crib with her favorite blankie, and Jax was on the road. The visit at Chase's foster home was brief, but it confirmed the little guy was recovering from a cold. His foster parents thought he would be able to return to day care in the morning. Jax called Naomi at Little Blessings with the update and asked that the message be passed along to Serena. Then he headed downtown to his office and worked a few hours on court filings and briefs.

When the clock had finally crept past the time for Daci and Serena's shift to end, he called Daci's cell. She answered after two rings.

"Where are you?" he asked.

"At the office, updating DC Reynolds on our activities today. He told me the woman I knocked over in the crosswalk yesterday was treated and released. No bones broken."

"I'm thankful for that. Just wondering if you wanted to join me for a drive-by of Serena's apartment building. Maybe do a little recon of the area, too."

A brief chuckle answered him. "Been there, done that. Plus, I'm picking Serena up at her place at six thirty. We're attending a recovery meeting together tonight."

Jax let out a low whistle. "Fast work, rookie!"

She snorted. Odd how even that gruff sound was attractive coming from her.

"Not hard," she said, "with someone so needy for human companionship and approval."

"What's the address of the meeting? I'd like to hang around outside and watch for either our mutual friend or a go-between who might want to contact Serena outside of her work-place or residence."

"Good idea." Daci rattled off the address.

"What do you drive, so I'll know which vehicle is yours?"

"I've got a blue Volkswagen GTI. Blurs the line between sporty and utilitarian. Just the way I like it." She laughed.

Jax grinned as they ended the call. He'd expected at least a Lexus, if not a Mercedes, but a VW? She'd certainly pulled off the balance between maintaining her average-income profile with the flair of something slightly off the beaten path.

Two hours later, Jax parked up the block from Bethany Church in south Springfield, where the recovery meeting was being held. He had arrived early to monitor Daci and Serena's approach. If anyone was following them, he would spot the tail. He popped open the door on the glove compartment of his Malibu, took out his Glock 19 and checked the load.

Lying beneath the gun, his temporary marshal's badge caught his eye. Slowly, he hefted it in one palm, testing the familiar weight. Running the pad of his thumb across the gold star and embossed eagle, memories rushed through him. Hissing in a breath, he flung the badge back into the glove compartment and slammed it shut.

He lifted his gaze to find a shiny blue GTI turning the corner and approaching the church. The vehicle drove toward him, then entered the parking lot that was already filling up with those attending the meeting. Jax scanned the area for vehicles slowing down in surveillance mode or parked cars with occupants that seemed to be watching the church like he was. Nada.

He settled back in his seat for a bit of a wait. When the meeting was over, he was going to follow them back to Serena's apartment. Her part of town wasn't a good area to be in after dark. Not a good place to raise a child, either, but a rough neighborhood wouldn't be sufficient reason to deny Serena her son if she met the court-ordered criteria for custody. And at the moment, it was the best she could afford. Sometimes a person had to pick his battles.

The two hours until the meeting let out reminded Jax of how much he'd hated stakeout duty. At last, people began emerging from the church, Daci and Serena in the mix. Jax started his car, but let the VW get on up the road before he pulled out to follow. A few other vehicles from the meeting stayed with them for a while, but eventually, they all turned elsewhere.

Within twenty minutes, Daci pulled over near a corner lamppost in front of Serena's complex. Jax stopped at the curb on the opposite side of the street and watched as Daci got out with her charge. Had she already wangled an invitation up to Serena's apartment?

No, Serena stopped at the curb and seemed to be saying good-night. Daci lifted a hand in farewell and turned away as Serena went into her apartment building. Jax reached to put the Malibu in gear, then froze as a rust-bucket van cruised up the street and stopped in the middle of the road parallel with the VW. Jax's hair stood on end, every instinct screaming that Daci was in danger. He lunged for the gun in his glove compartment as the heavy rat-a-tat-tat of automatic weapon fire shredded the night.

THREE

A bullet buzzed past Daci's right ear as she dived behind the cover of her car. Heart pounding like a trip-hammer, she grabbed for the small pistol she'd strapped to her ankle for tonight's meeting. What good the little pea-shooter might do against an automatic was anybody's guess, but carrying her bulky service pistol hadn't been an option when she was undercover like this.

Abruptly, the staccato burst of gunfire ceased, and Daci popped her head up above the hood of her car for a quick look. With a screech of tires, the van raced away down the street. Daci got off a pair of shots, not expecting to hit anything more than the body of the van.

Other gunfire blended with hers, and her breath caught as she searched for the shooter. There! Jax was rushing up the middle of the road, pistol raised and blasting, but the van didn't slow down as it disappeared into the night.

Jax suddenly broke off chasing the fleeing vehicle, whirled and raced toward the bullet-riddled VW, calling her name. Panic edged his tone.

Daci jumped to her feet. "I'm here. I'm okay."

Jax trotted up her. "No, you're not. You're bleeding." He gestured toward her arm.

She glanced down. Sure enough. Warm blood trickled down her bare arm below the cap sleeve of her blouse. Now that the crisis was past, a hot burn in her biceps suddenly registered.

"Just a graze. Nothing serious."

"Nothing serious? Are you kidding? Some-one tried to kill you."

"Maybe they were gunning for Serena." Even as the words left her lips they felt false. The shooter had waited to spring until Serena went into the building. Daci *had* to be the tar-get, but why…and who was after her?

"We have to call this in."

The wail of sirens began closing in on their location.

Daci turned her head toward the shrill sound. "I think someone's already done that."

A half hour later, Daci wore a bandage over

the scratch on her arm, and for the second day in a row, she and Jax were answering the questions of a police detective. The people who lived in the surrounding apartment buildings remained noticeably absent, including Serena, though she must have heard the gunfire. Unfortunately, in this neighborhood shooting wasn't uncommon, and other than maybe anonymously calling the cops, the residents had learned to keep out of the way.

As Daci and Jax stepped away from the center of law-enforcement activity, Jax kept casting glances toward Serena's building. "Should we check on her?"

"The uniforms are casing the building for witnesses who may have been looking out their windows at the time of the shooting. That process will make a good cover for them to get eyes on her and leave us out of it. Especially you. She doesn't need to know you were here. I've asked the PD to call and advise me of her status as soon as they know it. I'll need a lift back to headquarters. My VW is now evidence at a crime scene."

"No problem. We both need to talk to Rey about the implications of you being the shooter's target."

"Couldn't it have been a random drive-by shooting?"

"Possible, I suppose."

By the tone of his voice, Jax didn't seem to find the suggestion probable.

"Could that mean I was also the intended victim of yesterday's attempted hit-and-run?" Letting the words out of her mouth brought a rank taste to Daci's tongue.

A grim mask settled over Jax's face. "A possibility we'll have to discuss."

Daci stared mutely out the window during the drive, and Jax seemed to get the hint that she didn't want to chat. If someone was trying to kill her, what impact might that circumstance have on her ability to do her job? Would she be pulled off her current case? While she'd been reluctant to take on this case from the start, when such a possibility loomed, she passionately wanted to finish the assignment, day care and all. It was her first assignment—she wanted to see it through. Wanted to prove herself. Would that chance be taken away from her?

Could she even be suspended from the service, pending apprehension of the culprit? Her gut curdled like the spoiled milk in the baby bottle she'd received in the mystery basket yesterday morning. She would have to tell her boss about that incident, also. A deep sigh left her throat.

"Hang in there." Jax reached over and squeezed her hand. "We're *going* to figure this out."

"Yes, we are."

Daci squared her shoulders. The determination in Jax's voice and the comfort of his touch shot fresh confidence through her veins. She'd fought through too much in her thirty-two years to allow this threat to derail her life just when she was getting it onto the track she wanted. She had to convince DC Reynolds that she could look after herself and Serena at the same time. Even better, either catch Liggett Naylor and jump-start her career, or expose the joker who was trying to put a final period on it. Best yet, do both!

Daci's ringtone sounded, and, following a brief chat with the officer on the other end, her heart lightened marginally.

She keyed off and smiled at Jax. "Serena's fine. Just rattled that she narrowly missed being out on the street when the shooting started."

He shot her a thumbs-up.

They found DC Reynolds in his office. He'd been called in immediately upon notification that a shooting incident involved one of his deputies. As they walked through his door, a double-deep scowl greeted them. Daci's gut churned.

"Sit!" he barked. They complied. "You okay, Marlowe?" he queried in a slightly less aggressive tone.

"I'm fine, sir." If only her nerves were as steady as the tone she'd managed.

"She's a trouper, Rey," Jax inserted.

Reynolds glared at him. "She's not a trooper. She's a deputy marshal, and I won't have some scum of the earth taking potshots at one of mine. So, what happened?" He switched his gaze to Daci.

She briefly summarized her evening with Serena, ending with the drive-by shooting. "Serena was in the building before the bullets flew, so she's okay."

Reynolds grunted. "Good thing." His desk chair squeaked as he leaned back and crossed his arms. "Now, about this shooting incident. If not for the attempted hit-and-run yesterday, I might be content to chalk it up to random gang activity in a rough neighborhood. But, taking the two incidents together, we may be looking at party or parties going after you personally, Marlowe. Who would want you dead?"

"I have no idea, sir. And you should know there has been a separate incident—a rather grotesque housewarming basket outside my door yesterday morning." She filled the men in on the contents of the basket and her failed attempts to uncover the culprit among her siblings.

Jax pulled a grimace and shook his head. "Some real practical jokers must be in your family if you thought they did it."

Daci shot him a sharp look. "You have no idea the pranks younger siblings will pull in an attempt to get a mothering—or, to their way of thinking, smothering—older sibling off their backs. The pranks got to be a habit, but as my brothers and sisters have grown into adulthood, I've always felt the love behind them. My sibs trying to pull one off and me catching them at it has become almost like a family tradition. This one felt different—more mean and crude than anything they'd do—but I didn't know who else to ask."

DC Reynolds's stare nailed Daci to her seat. "Then I suggest you begin sifting through your past to find another suspect. We don't need you distracted from your duties or drawing added danger to the assignment."

"You mean you don't want Serena catching a bullet or a bumper meant for me."

"I mean I want to catch Liggett Naylor, and I don't want to lose a deputy or a civilian as collateral damage to a murderous unsub unconnected to the case."

Jax cleared his throat. "There's another possibility." All eyes went to him. "Maybe the attempts on Daci's life *are* connected to the case. Is it possible Naylor found out she's a deputy marshal working undercover and wants to get her out from between him and Serena?"

Reynolds pursed his mouth. "Your theory isn't as bad as I'd like it to be."

Daci frowned. "I could see the shooting tonight coming from someone who didn't want me getting too close to Serena, but the basket and the hit-and-run came before I even met her."

"Before you met her, sure." Her boss nodded. "But not before the decision was made to give you this assignment. That happened two days ago. Keep your lips glued shut about this, but there must be a leak somewhere in the system in order for Naylor to have engineered his escape from custody in the first place. Could that mole know about Daci as a newb in the service assigned to his ex? As close to the vest as I've kept this operation, I doubt it, but I can't rule out the possibility. However, that theory still doesn't explain the gift basket. Not Naylor's MO at all. Too creative, and he never bothers to taunt his victims, just kills them."

"The basket could be unconnected to the attempts on my life," Daci said.

Reynolds sighed. "The operative word is *could*. For now, I'm willing to go with the benefit of the doubt that this may not be a personal vendetta against you. But keep a sharp eye out for yourself, because for whatever reason, someone wants you dead."

Daci leaned forward, excitement sparking. "If we assume I'm being targeted because Naylor knows I'm a deputy marshal, then he must be planning to contact Serena. That's a good thing, right?"

Jax let out a deep groan. "No, it's a bad thing, because the attempts on your life will continue. Are you sure it's wise to keep her on the assignment, Rey?"

Daci glared at Jax. "If my cover is blown because of a mole, then the mole will also expose anyone else assigned to Serena. The attacks won't stop—they'll just have a new target. I find it unacceptable to allow someone else to step in when I'm already in place and gaining her trust." She turned toward her boss. "Sir, I'm ready to return to duty at the day care in the morning."

Reynolds looked at his watch. "It's already morning. You'd better get home and sleep fast. Take an unmarked from the carpool until you get your own wheels back." He dug in his desk, pulled out a set of keys and tossed them her way.

As she caught the keys, Daci's insides did cartwheels. Her boss wasn't going to yank her from the case. Not yet, anyway. She headed for the door before the DC could change his mind. Jax followed on her heels.

She rounded on him in the deserted bull pen. "What's with urging DC Reynolds to take me off the case?"

His brows jerked together. "I wasn't *urging* anything that didn't need to be considered."

"Fine." The word was clipped as she struggled to rein in her temper. "But if we're going to work together," she poked his chest with a forefinger, "you can't start kid-gloving me."

Jax raised his hands, palms out. "Far be it, but would it offend you if I offered to walk you to your substitute wheels? As you know, my car is in the same ramp."

Daci's scowl lost the battle to a reluctant smile. "How about we walk each other? Anyone can use backup in the middle of the night in the heart of the city."

"Deal."

Outside, they found the usually busy Main Street almost deserted and as silent as a metro area ever became. The sky was clear and the breeze cool. Daci shivered slightly. Small talk about the Boston Celtics basketball season that had ended a few weeks past and the prospects for the next season occupied their brisk walk to Tower Square. Since basketball was invented in Massachusetts—in Springfield, to be specific—the game was a state obsession. But even as the idle conversation continued, the back of Daci's mind kept picking at the puzzle of the attempts on her life.

"You're wrestling with the who and why questions," Jax said softly into a silence Daci hadn't realized had fallen.

She nodded. "If it's not Naylor, who is coming after me and why?"

"Good questions. We've all got a past. What's in yours?"

They entered the parking garage, and their footsteps sounded hollow in the cavernous area—nearly as hollow as Daci's heart had suddenly gone. The question had sounded a little too knowing. She had no doubt this man had done extracurricular homework on her. How she hated that so many of the most painful parts of her life had been reduced to tabloid fodder that anyone could access! She'd spent the past fourteen years living under the radar in hopes her inner scars would heal and the world would forget about her and her tragic family.

Daci stopped beside the nondescript car she'd been issued. "Don't pretend you don't know." She glared up at him and found no denial on his face. He *had* looked into her history. "I do have violence in my past. A drug-crazed maniac slaughtered my parents, and seven others, at a wild party. Thankfully, I wasn't anywhere near that event, and the perp is behind bars. I know. I check often to make sure he's still locked away."

She turned and punched the button on the key fob to unlock the vehicle's door. "Two years later, a carjacker murdered my grandmother, who had been appointed guardian to my siblings and me. That time, I was an eyewitness. The perp got away and has never been seen or heard from again. But that happened years ago. If he was worried about my potential testimony against him, why has he waited until now to come after me?"

"Maybe something changed that suddenly made your silence vital."

"Come on! The time delay doesn't make sense. It's dead-end thinking." She yanked the car door open.

Jax stepped forward, blocking her access to the driver's seat. "I'm making it my personal business to ensure the phrase 'dead end' doesn't apply to you. I can't take another…"

"Another what?"

He stepped back, expression closed and hard. "Look *me* up on the internet. You'll find out that life and the news media haven't been kind to either of us."

He turned and strode away, and Daci's anger faded. A great weariness slumped her shoulders. She shouldn't have snapped at Jax like that, but thinking about that terrible carjacking always left her upset. Not only had she lost her beloved Grandma Katie in the attack, but had earned the enmity of her grandmother's only remaining child.

Uncle Conrad had always resented his sister marrying into an abundance of wealth and social status, completely overlooking the wreck his sister's life had become or the exploitations and injustices those very things had caused for Daci and her siblings. After his mother died at the hands of a carjacker trying to boost the Lexus she and Daci had driven to the grocery store, Con spewed venom, blaming Daci's "fancy-schmancy" car for drawing the notice of the thief. She'd marked the extreme reaction down to grief. Her uncle had apologized later for his words, but the accompanying request for money had pretty much voided the apology.

Yes, it was possible Con still hated her, but she couldn't wrap her head around him attempting to murder her. Long experience had revealed him to be a small and petty man, forever whining about injustices done to him, but not motivated to take action. Even if she took the idea seriously, a problem presented itself. As with the possibility of the carjacker being the one behind the attempted hit-and-run and the drive-by shooting, why wait until now to come after her?

Daci's knuckles whitened around the steering wheel. Connecting the attacks against her with something from her past was like trying to bang through a wall with her head. The simplest explanation was Liggett Naylor trying to get her out of the way to clear his path to his ex-girlfriend, but even that theory had holes.

By the time she reached her apartment, Daci's brain was sputtering on empty. Everything needed to take a back seat to slumber, even satisfying her curiosity about Jax. She bypassed her laptop and headed for her bedroom. Her head hit the pillow, and she was out, but the alarm rang immediately—or so it seemed. She staggered to the shower and got ready for her undercover job.

Less than an hour later, Daci stepped into the central play area at Little Blessings, sucking down the last gulp of the double espresso macchiato she'd picked up at a drive-through, along with a breakfast biscuit. After such meager sleep, the prospect of a day of diapers and spit-up, with a recovering addict in the mix, had required serious fortification. None of the children had arrived yet, but they could be expected to start trickling then flooding in at any moment.

Serena rushed up to her, wringing her hands. "Do you think Chase will be here today? What if he doesn't remember me? I've only been able to see him a few times since he was born. What happened to you?" She gestured toward the bandage on Daci's biceps, peeping out beneath the sleeve of the day care's polo shirt.

Daci opened her mouth, then shut it. Which question should she answer first? Might as well start with the last one and get that potential awkwardness cleared up.

"I didn't quite miss the drive-by shooting outside your apartment last night."

Serena's jaw dropped. "Oh, no! I assumed you were gone."

"Don't worry about it. Just a nick. Didn't even have to go to the hospital."

"I'll bet it hurts, though." Serena shuddered visibly. "Are you sure you should be here today? Maybe you have—like—PTSD or something."

Daci smothered a wry smile. "If I don't have

post-traumatic stress disorder by this point in my life, I'm unlikely to develop it. As for Chase coming to day care today and remembering you, I don't—"

"The children are starting to arrive!" The cheerful voice of Luvleen Drummond, the lead teacher for the babies, drew their attention toward the front door.

Within five minutes Serena's questions about Chase were satisfactorily answered. Mother cradled son and cooed at him as she carried him into the infant area. Daci followed with precious little Annie from the day before. She got the little girl happily situated on the floor with a few toys. Time to make Chase's acquaintance. Her gut clenched. Would she be able to tolerate Serena once she came face-to-face with the consequences the woman's alcohol consumption had wrought in utero on a developing baby?

"Introduce me to your son," she said as she walked up to Serena.

Beaming, the younger woman held Chase up for inspection. At first glance, the chubby six-month-old looked normal, but as Daci peered closer, she picked up on outward signs of the ongoing challenges the little guy—and his mother, provided she could hack it—would face.

The wobbly way the child held up his head

seemed more in keeping with a three-month-old than a six-month-old. And the flat face, almost nonexistent upper lip, and small eyes with epicanthal folds at the inner corners were all classic physical symptoms. Even though it might make things more difficult for Chase and Serena in some ways, she was glad the physical signs were there—visible and distinctive. They meant that he had been diagnosed at birth, which was truly the best-case scenario for him. Fetal alcohol syndrome did not reverse or improve with time. The earlier the learning disabilities and behavioral issues were anticipated and interventions put into place the better his life might turn out over the long term.

Daci dredged up a smile and tickled the little guy under the rolls of his pudgy chin. In response, a toothless grin slowly formed, and he gurgled and kicked. She lifted her gaze to Serena's. Behind the young woman's bright smile, stark terror lurked.

Of what or whom was she afraid? Herself? Did she doubt her ability to lead a sober life or her capacity to cope with her child's problems? Both or either would be understandable, but Daci had already learned not to leap to logical conclusions where Serena was concerned.

The younger woman leaned close to Daci. "Do you think he's cute? I think he's adorable."

Seriously? The woman was afraid people wouldn't find Chase attractive? Outward appearance was what concerned her most?

"If anybody disses my boy," Serena went on fiercely, "because of the way he looks or stuff he does or 'cause he takes a little extra time to figure things out, I will totally wear them out."

A chuckle worked its way past Daci's lips. Now, there was the mama bear. She could respect that.

"He absolutely *is* adorable. Let me hold him." Daci held out her arms.

Maybe she hadn't been given the chance to protect Niall, but she had the golden opportunity to defend this little guy and his mama from a vicious predator, and that is just what she was going to do, so help her God!

The judge's stare from the bench seared through Jax. Had he messed up his opening argument that badly? The judge tapped the side of his jaw and nodded toward him. Jax's brows drew together. The judge tapped again. Jax reached up and felt the side of his chin. Warmth bathed his face as he pulled away the tiny square of toilet tissue from the spot he'd cut himself while shaving this morning. He offered the judge a small grin. The man's eyes twinkled as he looked away to call for opposing counsel's opening argument.

Jax settled into his chair, thankful this was not a jury trial; otherwise, twelve citizens he'd never met before would be mentally assigning him to the clown department. At least this judge, upon whom rested the fate of his very young client, knew him to be a competent attorney. Usually.

Today, as opposing counsel droned on, Jax's thoughts went to Daci Marlowe and their conversation of only a few hours past. Who was trying to kill her? Naylor? The prospect made a degree of sense, but, if so, it was the only activity from him since he'd escaped. All of the former crime boss's known associates had been shaken down hard, but each one adamantly denied seeing or hearing from him. Naylor appeared to have vanished without the proverbial trace.

As troubling as that development was to the US Marshals Service, Jax was infinitely more disturbed by the attacks on Daci. What if another attempt was made—this time successful? No, he wouldn't let that happen. Not on his watch!

Jax shook his head. Who was he trying to fool? He hadn't been able to protect Regan or his unborn child. What made him think he could protect Daci?

An hour later, following satisfactory disposition of his case, he was on his way toward the day care to look in on Chase as a pretext to check on Daci. No one would think it odd that he dropped in to follow up on a baby that had been out ill the day before. Maybe he could grab a chance to talk to Daci privately.

He parked at the curb and went inside, greeting familiar workers as he went. In the infant play area, he found Daci with her hands full, playing with five little ones. Through an observation window into the next room, he spotted two other workers feeding and changing additional babies. The lead teacher was with Serena and Chase at a corner table. Daci was clearly not free to talk, so he joined Serena and Luvleen.

From the activity going on with a small rattle, Jax deduced the middle-aged black woman was teaching the younger woman how to work with her son on developing the motor skills necessary for grasping and holding on to objects. Luvleen's every movement conveyed calming grace, exactly what these troubled infants required, and an art the jittery Serena must absorb for the sake of her child.

"Hello, Jax." Serena greeted him coolly, a

far cry from the needy enthusiasm of yesterday and probably more in keeping with her true feelings toward him.

"Is Chase doing all right today?"

"He's here, isn't he?"

Luvleen sent him an apologetic glance through thick-lensed glasses. "We're just finishing our session. Do you need a minute to confer with Serena?"

The younger woman's facial features tensed even as she scooped her son out of the infant seat.

"Not necessary," Jax answered. "I can see there are good things going on here."

Serena's shoulders relaxed visibly. "It's Chase's nap time anyway. I'm going to change and feed him, then put him down in his crib."

"Sounds good," Luvleen said. "Then take over for Daci so she can go on her break."

Serena nodded and whisked Chase away.

"Have you met our other new worker?" Luvleen nodded toward Daci, who had her charges arranged in infant seats in a semicircle on the floor around her and was singing a silly song with actions. "She's amazing, isn't she? What a find! We badly need at least one more attendant in this area. Do you know of anyone?"

Jax was only half listening after the word *amazing*. Watching Daci interact with the little ones was fascinating. How could she keep the rapt attention of five less-than-one-year-olds? Yet they all gazed up at her, some of them kicking and chortling, as she sang her ditty in a soft, throaty voice.

"Do you?" Luvleen repeated.

"What? Oh." Jax blinked down at her. "No, sorry, I don't. And, yes, I met Daci yesterday when I dropped in to see Annie—and Chase, but he was out ill."

"That's right. Naomi told me you stopped by while I was performing one-on-one therapy."

"How is Chase coming along? Do you think he'll be able to bond with his mother?"

"Too soon to say, though I can testify that Serena is doing her best to make that happen. Time will tell if her commitment will last. FAS babies are difficult for even well-adjusted adults to handle. The only edge she's got going for her is mother love, and I never underestimate the power of that."

Jax smiled and nodded, still riveted by Daci's interaction with the children. "I guess that's it for me here, then. Thanks. I have a couple other clients to see in the toddler rooms."

On reluctant feet, he left the area without talking to his partner. Jax spent a half hour chatting with other caregivers and getting down on the floor to play with his little clients. As far as he was concerned, this was the best part of the job.

A soft laugh behind him drew his attention. He looked over his shoulder to find Daci gazing down at him in the act of building a block tower with a toddler.

"I like what I see," she said. "No one can say you don't spend quality time with your clients."

He grinned. "I like what I see, too." His face heated as her mouth slackened into an O. "I mean, I liked watching you interact with the kids."

Her eyes lit in an expression that could only be called mischievous. "So, you don't like what you see now, just what you saw then? A girl could get a complex."

"Sure, go ahead and give me the old razzamatazz for a slip of the tongue."

She laughed and his skin tingled. If he didn't know better, he'd think they might be flirting. Good thing he knew better. Right?

She dropped down cross-legged between him and the tot. "I've got a few minutes left of my break."

Together, the three of them finished the tower. Then Daci and he laughed and clapped as the little guy gleefully demolished it. A yawn overtook Jax in the midst of the clapping, and he covered his mouth.

"Sleepy, Williams? We have an open crib."

He smirked. "Kind offer, but my best blankie is at home."

Daci checked her watch. "Oops, I'm overdue back at my station."

"And I'm due in court soon. Talk to you later."

"For sure." She waved and hustled off.

As Jax headed back to his car parked a short way up the street, he stifled another yawn. Some major caffeine mojo might be in order. If his brain continued in its current mushy condition, he could drop the ball on his pint-size client during trial. Not acceptable.

Jax reach for the Malibu's door handle, but a shrill alarm arrested him. He whirled toward the day care. The alarm continued to blare, and the glass doors of the facility erupted open. Workers and their charges poured out. Fire alarm? He sniffed the air and studied the building. No smoke. But lack of smoke noticeable from this vantage point didn't mean there was no fire.

He raced toward the center to offer assistance. Some of the little ones milling around on the lawn were crying and trembling, but at least they were safe. Anyone still inside might not be. Bucking the outflow, Jax plunged into the building, gaze searching frantically for

Daci, Serena and little Chase. For that matter, he hadn't seen Luvleen emerge, either. The rush of exiting bodies was slowing to a trickle, but there was still no sign of them. If Liggett Naylor or some faceless threat to Daci had arranged a distraction in order to get to them, this was perfect.

Sniffing for telltale smoke but still not detecting any, Jax trotted for the infant section. Heart hammering against his ribs, he burst into that area to find it empty. Unless they were in one of the changing or crib rooms. Calling their names, he began throwing open doors but discovered no occupants. Where could they have gone? Had he missed them in the melee outside?

Racking his brain, he took a side door and found himself in a hallway across from a few offices at the rear of the building. The shrill screech of the alarm beat against his ears, but, even louder and higher, a female shriek raked his nerve endings. The noise came from beyond the metal door at the end of the hallway. Of course! Workers would be trained to get the children out the nearest exit. At this end of the building, that exit would be in the back.

Jax raced up the short hallway and burst through a door labeled Emergency Exit Only.

His feet ground to a halt in the gravel of the employee parking lot.

Several small children huddled together in Luvleen's embrace. Another worker cradled a pair of infants. A third held a baby while speaking rapidly into a cell phone.

A few feet beyond them, near an idling car, Serena shrieked as she pounded at the beefy back of a man who clutched a wailing Chase. The infant dangled from one of the man's arms, while he used the other to try and dislodge Daci's two-handed grip on his shirt that prevented him from ducking into the open driver's door of the vehicle. Even as Jax plunged into motion, the man drew back his fist for a roundhouse punch headed straight into Daci's face.

FOUR

Daci ducked beneath the sweeping blow, the air current from the flying fist ruffling her hair. Off balance, the man staggered even as Daci snatched Chase from the abductor's loosened grip. She darted away as a freight train in the form of a lean, charging figure slammed the culprit to the ground.

The fire alarm abruptly ceased, but not the bedlam outside. The abductor on the ground bellowed curses as Jax fastened his arms behind his back with a zip tie pulled from his suit jacket pocket. The man definitely came prepared for anything. Still screaming, Serena rushed in, grabbed a howling Chase, and hugged him to her heaving chest, while the other small children squealed and wailed in chorus.

Since Jax had the perp under control, Daci turned and wrapped her arms around Serena and her baby. "Hush, now. Hush, hush. It's all over."

The young woman's cries subsided into ragged breathing. "Why would…some stranger… try to steal Chase? Unless…no, he wouldn't!"

"Who wouldn't?" Daci looked Serena in the face.

The woman's gaze went stony, and her chin jutted as she clamped her jaw shut. Daci tamped down her disappointment. Apparently, it was still too soon to presume she had Serena's confidence.

"Never mind." Daci patted her arm. "Focus on comforting Chase."

The young woman nodded and began cooing and rocking her son, who was letting out hoarse squawks and alternately doubling up and stiffening straight out.

With Serena completely engaged with her son, Daci turned away to find Jax still on the ground with his knee pinning the would-be abductor's back. The man lay still and silent now as Jax leaned close to his ear, speaking in tones too quiet for Daci to make out words. Was he questioning the attacker? This was probably their only shot at interrogating the guy before the PD got their hands on him. The Marshals Service would likely send in an interrogator of their own when they got him to lockup, but it wouldn't be either Jax or her because they still had to protect their undercover status, unless or until they knew for certain it was blown.

The bellow of sirens closed in on their location. Police and firefighters converged on the scene. The police took the perp into custody, and firefighters soon declared the day care building safe. Day care staff, including Daci, concentrated on returning the children to their normal environment and activities while being pulled aside, one by one, for brief interviews by the investigators. Naomi disappeared into her office to call parents, who were required to be notified of the emergency, though the fire had been a false alarm.

The question on the top of Daci's mind was who had activated the alarm. The would-be abductor couldn't have done it because he didn't have access to the interior of the day care. The only way *into* the building, since the emergency-exit doors were locked for ingress but open to egress, was through the front door. Security there was rigid under the watchful eyes of Naomi Minch and Emma Tyse, the no-nonsense clerical assistant who rarely budged from behind the front desk. No, the perp had been waiting out back to snatch his prey, which meant someone on the inside had pulled the alarm switch at a time when that person knew

Chase would be in an area of the building that would necessitate evacuating him out the rear door.

Daci's gaze traveled the play area. Was it petite Hayley, who supervised a group of three children at the sand table? Or maybe Jose, the wide-as-he-was-tall toddler teacher currently fitting aprons onto four tiny pupils about to start finger painting? What about other workers who weren't directly in her line of sight? Luvleen? Never! Daci's faith in her ability to judge character would be forever shattered. Could it be Cecil or Wendy or Marina or Takisha or others she hadn't met yet? She didn't know any of them well enough to have an opinion about who might be enticed to betray an infant. Her blood boiled at the thought.

A tall figure entered the room and stopped beside her. "I envy children's ability to so quickly leave the ugly behind and enjoy themselves again." He nodded around the room at all the happy activity and laughter.

"Me, too." Was her tone as wistful as she felt? "I think I must have been born with a hyperactive responsibility gene because I don't remember ever being this carefree."

Jax frowned but let the comment slide, and Daci was grateful. What had possessed her to blurt out such a personally revealing remark?

"I hate to say it," he murmured, "but one of the staff here had to have been in on this abduction attempt."

"Agreed." She kept her voice low, also. The walls might not have ears, but the people bustling around had two each. "All workers have their backgrounds checked before coming on board, but we need to dig deeper on each of them. Maybe someone has a new personal association or problem that has left them open to coercion. Did the perp tell you anything?"

"Nothing except grumbling about finding an easier way to pay a debt. I said, 'Depends on who you owe.' He answered, 'You don't mess with this guy. You do what he says.' The remark points to Naylor, don't you think?"

"Strong indication. Which means he could still be in the area if the perp's assignment was to bring him his son."

"Or he could be in Timbuktu, having arranged remotely for the grab and delivery. Hopefully, we'll know more later today, after the PD and the Marshals Service get done grilling our would-be baby-snatcher. In the meantime, I hate to leave, but I have to be in court in less than an hour."

"No time to change your pants, then, I guess."

"Huh?"

Daci dropped her gaze to the slit of skin peeking between the rent in Jax's suit pants over the left knee.

He followed her look and let out a groan. "This morning it was TP on a shaving cut. This afternoon it's a rip in my pants. Same judge, too. He's going to think I've lost my mind."

"Not if you explain you were going above and beyond to save an infant."

"You were the one who grabbed Chase. Nice bob and weave, by the way."

Daci's insides warmed, and a smile crept onto her lips. "Thanks. We can call it a team effort."

"I like that." Their gazes locked and held as Jax's grin mirrored hers.

Her heart rate swept into overdrive, and she hastily tore her gaze away.

Clearing his throat, Jax looked away, also. "Connect with you downtown later." He lifted a hand in farewell.

Daci's gaze followed his retreating back as he left the building. That confident stride and the straight set of his shoulders indicated a man of determination. His actions had proved courage, and his choice of career—as well as how he carried it out—displayed compassion and integrity. So many admirable qualities made him too attractive for her peace of mind.

The gravitational pull between them was intense. His body language said he felt the same way and fought it like she did. She knew why *she* resisted. The timing couldn't be worse for romance when she was trying to get her career underway. And how unprofessional would it be to allow attraction to muddy her thoughts about a colleague when they were on a case together? Was professionalism his reasoning, also? Maybe in part, but she sensed something much deeper and very painful throwing up a wall between them. Maybe it was time she took his invitation and looked into his background.

But right now she needed to check on Serena and Chase. She found the younger woman in the dim and quiet nap area, sitting beside her son's crib and watching the little boy sleep.

At Daci's approach, the younger woman turned a face of misery toward her. "His foster parents are coming to get him. I won't even be able to hold him if he wakes up and cries again."

Daci laid a hand on Serena's slumped shoulder and squeezed. It was getting easier to feel genuine sympathy for Serena, but then, it had been easy to feel sympathetic toward her mother or father when they were in their rare sober moments and lamenting the consequences of their lifestyle. But momentary remorse never led to true repentance or substantial change, and the cycle of substance abuse and child neglect soon began all over again.

At one point, Grandma Katie had tried to have Daci and her siblings removed to her custody, but that hadn't happened until her parents were dead and there was no one else, with the exception of Uncle Conrad. Thankfully, Uncle Con's DUI record eliminated him from the court's consideration. But as long as Daci's parents were alive, her father's old Boston money and prestige of name had spoken too loudly for the courts to hear anything else—not from a working-class, first-generation Swiss immigrant like her grandmother, who still spoke English with a pronounced accent.

Part of Daci's parents' psychosis as addicts was delusional pride in their parenting. They liked to tell everyone they looked after their children personally. What that meant in reality was that they neglected their children while refusing to hire proper caregivers. They made an exception when the twins were born and hired a day nanny to help out for a year and a half or so, but even then, four-year-old Daci changed more diapers and fed more bottles than both of their parents combined—often in the middle of the night when the adults in the house were passed out and the babies were crying. Over the years, as more children came along, various cooks and housekeepers went beyond their assigned duties and helped with physical cares.

But Grandma Katie with her warm letters and frequent visits and taking Daci and her siblings to church—when their mother and father allowed the outing—had provided the totality of the adult, familial affection Daci received when she was very small. Later, after Grandma had unsuccessfully sued for custody and was barred from the house, only the letters remained to comfort and sustain Daci through some very rough times.

In Serena's case, the young woman had neither money nor name going for her, but the courts were considering returning her irreversibly damaged son to her dubious motherly care—and Jax was deeply involved with that system. Another compelling reason to resist her attraction to the man. A relationship with him could drive her insane with aggravation every time he lamented when poor judgments were rendered for tiny clients. Because sometimes, as she well knew, the system simply didn't work.

Daci pulled her hand from Serena's shoulder. "I gather you didn't know the man who tried to take your son. You called him a 'stranger.' Do you think Chase was targeted or was the guy after any random child?"

Serena rose and motioned for Daci to follow her to the corner of the room away from the crib. Pulse quickening, Daci complied.

The younger woman leaned close to Daci's ear. "You saved Chase out there, so I guess I owe it to you to be on the level." Serena's gaze darted around like she thought someone could be skulking in the shadows. "It's gotta be tied to my ex-boyfriend. You know? He's a menace. I'll bet he sent one of his crooked buddies to get Chase."

"Chase's father wants custody? Has he tried through the court system?" Daci all but held her breath to see what insights her innocent-sounding fishing questions might draw out.

"The court system!" Serena snorted. "Yeah, the law wants him real bad. Back behind bars where he belongs! I figured him and me were quits. I never guessed he'd care a snap about any kid he had, much less one with me, one that wasn't…like…all right. You know?"

"Does he know Chase has FAS?"

"I doubt it." The younger woman shook her head. "I didn't even know he knew he had a son! But the bad dude's got resources, let me tell you."

"Has he tried to contact you?" Daci prayed the extreme urgency in her heart hadn't bled through into her tone. She didn't need to spook Serena now.

The younger woman's gaze dropped away, and she wriggled in that nervous mannerism of hers. "Not directly."

"What does that mean?"

Serena jerked her head up, her gaze hard and fierce. "I just have this feeling like I'm being watched all the time, but now that someone has come after Chase, I'm sure he's out there waiting like a big, nasty spider in one of his hidey-holes."

"Serena! For your own safety and Chase's, if you know where this guy is you need to tell the authorities."

"I did that once, and they let him get away. Now he's on the loose again. He must not know that I told before, or I'd be dead already. I'm sober now and in control of my lips. I won't risk opening them again, even if I knew where he is, which I don't. And you better not tell any cops what I said, either. Not if you care about me and Chase…or your own life. That man doesn't care who he hurts."

The baby mewled and started to fuss. Serena whirled and stalked toward the crib. Frowning, Daci watched the younger woman. All Serena's defensive anger melted away as she bent over the crib, crooning to her son. Daci's heart broke. Serena was no one's idea of a model mother, but that she loved her son there was no doubt. Would that love be enough to keep her sober? Would the dangerous connections from her past allow her to live long enough to find out?

What about dangerous connections from Daci's own turbulent history? Was someone in the shadows of her past bent on ending her career and her life? Other than her grandmother's killer, there was only one other person she could think of who might have a reason to want her dead. Did Uncle Conrad hate her that much? But why come after her now?

She would have to pay him a visit—look him squarely in the eyes and find out how deep his resentment ran. But she wasn't going alone into that confrontation. Someone needed to be there to verify what was said and done, but she didn't want to get any of her siblings involved in raking up this muck. Only one person appeared in her mind's eye as an appropriate, objective witness—Jaxton Williams.

"Where does your Uncle Conrad live?" Jax asked Daci as they sat together at her desk, going over the day's events, as well as speculations about her angry uncle.

The guy sounded like a prize jerk, blaming Daci for his mother's death just because she had an expensive car. Might be the reason Daci drove a VW now. Of course, grief did a number on people's capacity for decency and sound reason. The guy might have his head screwed on better by now, but it was a good idea to take a close look at him.

"Uncle Con lives in the Mid Dorchester neighborhood of Boston," Daci answered.

"That's a couple of hours away on I-90. He could be behind your delightful gift basket, if nothing else."

Daci let out a dry chuckle. "Actually, the gift basket thing sounds more his speed than attempted murder, but I haven't shared my new address with him, or told him about my job. Whoever left that basket had to know where I moved only a week ago, and when I was starting work."

"Narrows the suspect pool considerably." Jax frowned. "Only leaves people in this office who can access your file, or family and friends you notified—unless they passed the information along to someone."

"Not too likely. Everyone in the family/ friend category knows how protective Marlowes are of our personal information. But, look, I don't want investigating my funky family to steal time from our assignment in the Liggett Naylor case. Would you be willing to go to Boston with me some evening after duty hours or even this weekend? I mean, strictly business. DC Reynolds did say to get a handle on who might be after me, in case it turns out not to be Naylor. I don't want to steal your free time, though, so—"

Jax laid his forefinger across Daci's mouth. She'd spoken faster and faster, and her face had gone progressively redder with every word.

"No worries," he said. "I definitely want to go with you. I'm honored you asked. I'd say the sooner the better." He looked at his watch. "How about we grab some fast food at a drive-through and head out?"

"Hole in the knee and all?" She grinned down at the rent in his pants. "What did the judge say?"

"Not a word. I stayed behind my table and played innocent the whole time and may have hit a home run for my tiny client, but the decision won't be handed down until later this week. And as for meeting your uncle, given what you say about the guy's attitude, I don't think impressing him with my sartorial elegance needs to be a concern. Maybe you should call and make sure he's home?"

Daci shook her head. "I don't want to warn him I'm on the way. People's reactions are more revealing when they're spontaneous. He's an auto mechanic who likes to hang out with his bar buddies. When Con isn't at work, he's at home glued to ESPN or hoisting more than a few at the local sports bar. We'll try home first. He's an avid sports gambler, which is the biggest reason I rarely give him any cash when he hits me up."

"How often is that?" Jax scowled.

She rolled one shoulder in a shrug. "Not often. He figured out pretty quickly that blaming me for his mother's death wasn't going to guilt me into coughing up green every time his team lost. Three years back, I bought him a new car when his old rust bucket gave out on him, but then he got in a fender bender about six months ago, and come to find out, he had no insurance because he'd gambled away the money to pay the premium. Needless to say, I refused to cover his fine or pay for the body work on the vehicle. He didn't take my decision well." Her mouth pulled into a grimace. "It's really too bad. If he was a solid, trustworthy guy I would give him the moon. He's family, after all."

A half hour later, Springfield was fading in their rearview mirror as they headed for Boston, Daci behind the wheel.

Jax polished off the last of his burger and wiped his fingers on a paper napkin. "I'm glad the PD has assigned an officer to live in with Chase's foster family and accompany them whenever they take Chase out of the house until the danger is past. With you stationed at the day care, and me in and out as much as possible, we should have the little guy covered."

Daci wrinkled her nose. "Especially since the day care worker who pulled the alarm for her abductor boyfriend won't be there anymore. Boy, is Marina in hot water."

"Deservedly so."

"Too bad they're both sticking to their claim that they don't know Naylor's whereabouts, and that the baby-snatching deal was set up by a go-between. I do worry about Serena, though. You and I have eyes on her during workday hours, and between the Marshals Service and PD, her building is staked out and her whereabouts are continually monitored, but we don't have anyone living with her. Someone could get to her. Plus, since she turned down protection, we can't even tell her someone's keeping an eye on her. She feels like she's facing this all on her own. That's got to be terrifying."

"Are you starting to be a little fond of Chase's mother?"

Daci shot him a glower. "I'm about as conflicted as a cat crouched between a mouse and a canary. Every molecule in me hates what her choices did to her son, yet I see she deeply regrets her behaviors and truly loves Chase. And no matter what she's done, no one deserves to be targeted by a killer like Naylor. I want to see her get through this safely, for her sake and for Chase's. But getting Naylor out of the picture won't solve all of her problems. Even if she successfully graduates from her halfway house, benefits from therapy and counseling, succeeds at her day care job, and gets her son back, she needs intensive monitoring and support for a few years, not merely a few months, to make sure the changes stick. Are there any programs out there that will fit the bill?"

Jax nodded. "A few, and I'll hook her up with those, but what they offer will still leave gaps—most prominently, the personal touch of a solid, platonic relationship to offer her support. A sober friend who loves and cares for her. She has no one. The woman was living on the streets by the age of fourteen after her parents booted her out. It's actually amazing she's not dead and still has a conscience."

"I know." Daci's tone was grim. "Her family background—or lack thereof—was in her file. I'm angry *for* her, not just *at* her, but don't get any ideas about setting me up as the permanent 'friend.' It's all I can do to handle this association as a work assignment."

Jax flung up his hands. "I would never presume to dictate your friendships."

Daci sniffed. "But you do have a persuasive way about you."

"Comes with the lawyer territory. I'm talking about charm, not smarm."

"You said it, buster."

He grinned. She didn't, but he detected an upward twitch of one corner of her mouth. Apparently, she wasn't entirely immune to the aforementioned charm.

Soon the Boston skyline painted a giant halo of light on the dusky horizon. Traffic trebled and then quadrupled. They turned off at one of the Mid Dorchester exits and entered a middle-to-lower income neighborhood of duplexes and cookie-cutter apartment buildings. Commercial streets consisted primarily of bars, mom-and-pop shops, ethnic restaurants and a scattering of so-called adult entertainment establishments. The male pedestrians wore casual to grubby day-laborer-type garb. The same with the women, except for a few sporting trashy nightclub bling. No trendy fashion to be seen.

A soft sigh exhaled from Daci. "Katerina Meier immigrated to this neighborhood in 1959 with her US Army husband. They met while he was on leave in Zurich. Ironically, she got to keep her maiden name, just spelled differently. My grandpa—who I never met— was named Rudolph Meyer. Tough break that Rudy died shortly after my mother was born."

Her tone was of one reminiscing aloud to herself, not someone making conversation. Jax held himself still and silent, willing her to go on.

"Katie was left a young widow with a three-year-old boy and a less-than-one-year-old daughter to raise. She worked hard, kept them fed and clothed, insisted they finish high school, encouraged them to move on to college for the education she so prized, but they both wanted to get the American Dream the easy way. Neither sought higher education, but my mother *exceeded* her goal of wealth and luxury through marriage to a man with big money and an old name. Con never got what he thought was due him. Now he's a bitter middle-aged man living alone in the same duplex where he grew up and working a job he only tolerates."

She suddenly glanced over at him as if realizing she had an audience for her musings.

He smiled. "Did your grandmother tell you this?"

She shook her head and navigated a turn around a corner by a mechanic shop that advertised cheap oil changes.

"My uncle works here." She waved toward the closed and dark building. "Mostly, I pieced the history together from things I overheard. Some of it came from my grandma, but quite a bit from my mother, who talked practically nonstop when she was in certain moods. The interpretation is my own."

"You were an attentive and observant child."

"I had to be."

"My childhood was oatmeal compared to yours, though it did involve a blended family. My mom passed away when I was very young, and my dad remarried a woman who also had a young child. I can't squawk about my stepmom, though. She's great! My stepsister and I aren't close, but we don't fight—at least not now that we're adults." He chuckled.

"Be thankful."

"I am, but even the Brady Bunch had their problems."

"No time for it now, but on our way home you can tell me about your problems, Mr. Brady." She laughed. "I need to have something on you after all the blathering I've done about my dirty laundry. I'm not usually so forthcoming. Must be because I sense no judgment in your listening."

The backs of Jax's eyes stung. If only he could allow himself to open up to this woman. He sensed the same sympathetic ear in her. But baring his soul would inevitably open the door of his heart, and he couldn't afford to let her in.

A law-enforcement career created risks for both of them—risks he could no longer accept in concert with a romantic relationship. His wife and unborn child had died because he was a marshal. The guilt of their loss was as great as the sorrow. If Daci and he were a couple, and a similar event occurred where he lost his life, she'd be left feeling like he did right now. Or he'd be left behind to mourn her. He could not allow either possibility. Denying any attraction for Daci, beyond coworker camaraderie, was the only right course.

"What is that smell?"

"Huh?" Her question broke him out of his introspection. He sniffed the air. "Smoke."

"We're getting close to my uncle's house."

She sped up and a few blocks later turned a corner. Dead ahead, fire trucks and police cars, lights flashing, surrounded the charred remains of a home.

Jax's gut clenched. "Your uncle's place?"

Her terse affirmative was accompanied an abrupt halt at the curb as close to the ordered chaos as they could get. Was that an ambulance among the emergency vehicles? Jax leaped from the car and raced to catch up with Daci, who was charging into the fray. Smoke hung acrid in the air as embers hissed at the water streaming from hoses trained on the wreckage.

Just as Jax caught up to his partner, a burly uniformed officer stepped into her path.

"No closer, ma'am. Authorized personnel only."

"I *am* authorized." She whipped out her badge.

The uniform squinted down at the deputy marshal ID, illuminated by a nearby floodlight. "Hey, Lieutenant Jacobs," he hollered to a man in a suit who stood, hands in pockets, near the idling ambulance. "Did you call in the US Marshals Service?"

The craggy-faced plainclothes detective removed his hands from his pockets, sauntered over and repeated the squint at Daci's badge. Jax hovered in the background. The fact that the ambulance emergency lights were not flashing and the paramedics sat on the rear bumper could be good news or bad. Either no one was injured…or the injuries were fatal, and there was no hurry.

"Lieutenant Ben Jacobs." The detective thrust a bony hand toward Daci, apparently satisfied with his inspection of her bona fides.

She shook the hand, then Jax shook it in his turn. "Marshals Service, also," he said.

"What happened here?" Daci clipped out.

"Why is the Marshals Service interested in a residential house fire?" Jacobs countered.

Daci waved toward the smoldering remains. "My uncle Conrad lives—er, lived there. Is he all right?"

The detective frowned. "If this is a personal visit, you shouldn't be flashing your badge."

"Yes…uh, no. Not a personal visit…but *now* it's personal. I need to know about my uncle!" Her hands fisted at her sides.

Jax had never seen Daci so flustered—not even when someone shot at her or tried to run her over in the street. Despite her pragmatic assessment of her uncle's character and the way he'd treated her, she really cared about the guy.

Jax stepped forward, pulling the attention away from his partner. "What can you tell us about the situation? Accident? Arson? Casualties?"

"We are reasonably certain no one was home in one of the duplexes. The fire was arson, no question. But it wasn't started until *after* the murder."

"Murder!" Daci went stiff.

Jax sidled closer to her. "Do you know the vic's identity?"

The detective's demeanor softened. "The ID on the man firefighters pulled from the blaze says Conrad Meyer. That your uncle?"

"How did he die?" Daci said in a choked voice.

Jacobs let out a soft huff. "I'm sorry to say, he took a bullet to the head."

Daci wilted into Jax. Fighting the urge to wrap her close, he settled for putting his arm around her shoulders. Her whole body trembled against him like she was gripped by fever chills.

What were the odds that this murder was unconnected to the attempts on Daci's life? Next to nil. The killer had tried to put Daci in her grave and succeeded with her uncle. What was going on and why? The reason had to be personal—and now that they knew her uncle was involved, that meant it had to be connected to her bizarre family. This perp intended to keep on coming until he extinguished the bold flame that was Daci.

Jax's pulse throbbed in his neck. The world needed more people like the strong young woman he hugged to his side. She felt so right there. So natural. His heart was in more danger than he'd been willing to admit, but at this moment he didn't care. After all she'd endured and overcome, some lowlife was not going to put her on a mortuary slab. He was going to hunt this creature down and pray that digging into the reason for these murderous attacks did not unearth secrets that would add more pain to Daci's world.

FIVE

Focus... Think... No, don't think. Just focus.

The litany of self-advice played in the back of Daci's mind as she absorbed the details of what had been discovered so far in the case. Lieutenant Jacobs—or Ben, as he gave her and Jax permission to call him—was completely forthcoming with them.

Investigating officers were running a canvas of the area, but so far none of the neighbors admitted to having heard a gunshot or seen anything or anyone unusual until someone across the street noticed the smoke around seven that evening and called the fire department. Neighbors had verified that the duplex next to Con's was vacant so the Boston PD were hopeful they wouldn't discover further casualties as they sorted through the rubble.

Feet squishing in the sodden ground, the lieutenant and the arson investigator led Jax and Daci around back of the house. The investigator panned a flashlight across the foundation, revealing scorched splash marks of accelerant applied to start the blaze.

"The perp wasn't trying to use the fire to hide the crime of murder, as would be more usual in these cases," the investigator said. "It was more like he was trying to call attention to what he'd done. Even left the body near the front door so it could be rescued before the fire got to it."

"Thoughtful killer." Ben's tone dripped sarcasm.

"Almost like he was trying to send a message." The investigator scratched his head. "But to whom?"

"Me." Daci's answer emerged a thin squeak.

"You!" Ben whirled toward her. "Why?"

Jax spread his hands. "Searching for that answer brought us here."

"Tell me more," the detective said.

Words clogged Daci's tight throat. Her uncle had been murdered! Possibly because of her! If only she had some idea why or, more specifically, who was responsible, she might be able to stop this madness.

Jax filled the cop in with a terse summary of the attempts on Daci's life over the past couple of days. He omitted reference to their current assignment of watchdogging Serena and

Chase. In light of this arson and murder, he clearly shared her growing conviction that the two cases—whoever was after her and the danger to Serena and Chase—were not connected. But where did that leave her effectiveness as a marshal?

"Interesting." The detective turned toward Daci. "Before we get too far ahead of ourselves, though, we'd like you to take a look at the body and confirm his identity. Do you think you're up for it?"

She must look as shell-shocked as she felt. Forcing a nod, she turned and slogged through the mush to the front yard. The EMTs were starting to load the sheet-covered gurney onto the ambulance for transport to the morgue.

The lead EMT stopped as ordered and peeled the sheet back from the body's head. Daci ceased to breathe. Her uncle's broad face looked normal, except for the dime-sized hole in the middle of the forehead. Right between the eyes.

"You don't want to see the back of the skull," the EMT said. "The exit wound is where the real damage happened."

"It's Uncle Conrad," she croaked, and whirled away.

Halfway across the yard, strong hands gripped her shoulders, turned her and pulled her close. Her face mashed into a firm chest that smelled of some kind of wood-spice soap.

"Let's go home," he said, releasing her.

She nodded wordlessly and allowed him to guide her back to the unmarked sedan.

"I'm driving." He held out a hand for the keys.

She handed them over without protest and climbed into the passenger seat.

"Talk to me, Jax," she said. "Not about this mess or the Naylor case, but I'll go crazy if we sit here in silence."

"Some of that quid pro quo you were asking for when we arrived in Boston?"

"That'll do. Might even interest me."

"Thanks. I appreciate that."

A forlorn laugh escaped her lips. "I meant it as a compliment. Right now, not much could distract me from the fact that my uncle died because someone wants me good and scared."

"Maybe your uncle got deep in debt to some lowlife bookie who threatened to kill him if he didn't pay up. Maybe Conrad promised you would cover the debt, and the bookie initiated the attacks to soften you up before your uncle asked for the money."

"Plausible scenario if my uncle weren't already dead. Why kill him before the milk's been squeezed out of the cow?"

"Good point, but how do you know Conrad wasn't involved some other way in whatever is causing someone to come after you?"

Daci opened her mouth, but no retort filled it. She snapped her jaw shut. What if Uncle Con *was* a party to this mysterious vendetta someone was trying to fulfill against her? Maybe his participation had become a threat to the killer, or Con was experiencing remorse and a desire to confess and had to be silenced? But these were speculations that had no evidence whatsoever to support them.

She shook herself. "I can't think that way. Not when I have to go home and call my siblings to tell them their uncle has been murdered. They're going to ask why, and I don't want any suspicion bleeding through my voice when I answer 'I don't know.' Not unless or until we have proof of Con's involvement in whatever is going on."

"What about the attempts on your life? Are you going to omit those when you talk to your siblings, too?"

A grand sigh escaped her chest. "You ask the thorniest questions. Anybody ever tell you you'd make a great investigator?"

Jax chuckled.

Daci sniffed and folded her arms across her chest. "Stick to the quid pro quo, okay?"

"What do you want to know?"

"Where do you come from? What was it like growing up in your family? What makes you *you*."

"A simple bio. I can do that. Glad it's nothing nosy."

His teasing tone eased the tension gripping her. Life could be bad sometimes, really bad, but she had to thank God for the light moments and the people who brought them. Maybe that's how Grandma got through all the disappointments and obstacles in her life, being thankful for the good. She'd certainly done her best to pass the sunshine on to her often-struggling eldest granddaughter. The least Daci could do was follow her example.

Who was she kidding? She was nothing like her grandmother. Grandma Katie had been serene. Full of faith. Always ready with a smile and a soothing word. While Daci... Everyone said she was too intense. Too serious. How did she change that? Should she? If she hadn't been like she was, what would have become of herself and her siblings in the environment where they were raised?

Someone had to make sure teeth were brushed, hair was combed, clothes were appropriate, that they showed up daily to school, and they didn't stay up all night playing video games and eating junk food. Someone had to read the bedtime stories and keep a watchful eye on the antics in the backyard pool. And later, as grade school gave way to middle-school ages, that same someone had to run interference when controlled substances were too handy in the house for sneaking a sip or a toke. That era ended with the passing of her parents, and all the drugs and liquor were purged from the house.

But other forms of testing set in with the media scrutiny after the grisly deaths and the court tussle to see who would become guardian to her sixteen-year-old self and four siblings. And then, her grandma had been gone—stolen from their lives a mere two years after coming to live with them—and today, Grandma Katie's remaining child had been taken in a death just as violent and cruel. A life cut short by the murderous impulses of another person. And that same person seemed to have marked her for a short life, as well.

Why does this keep happening to my family, God? I want to see the bright side, but I don't. Help me!

"Have you heard a word I've said?"

Jax's sharp tone broke into Daci's awareness. She sat up straight from the slump she'd fallen into.

"Sorry." She brushed an errant strand of hair behind her ear. "I really wanted to listen, but I sort of fell into thinking and...well, praying."

"Praying is good."

"Yes, but I don't do it very well or very often. Too self-sufficient."

"Come to church with me on Sunday. You'd love my pastor. He's as down-to-earth as they come, great sense of humor, but boy, does he shoot God's Word straight to the heart."

"He sounds wonderful, but no thanks." She made herself ignore the disappointment in his eyes. "Tomorrow's Saturday—no day care— but I'm going to have to report my uncle's murder to DC Reynolds. I think that chat can wait until morning. Who knows whether I will get to stay on the Naylor case or not. In any event, my sibs and I will probably need the weekend to plan Uncle Conrad's funeral."

"Understandable, but let me know if you change your mind." He shot her a lopsided smile.

"Will do, Mr. Persistent."

"Part of my charm."

A laugh sneaked past her lips. "Did I hear you mention something about a frog and a mud puddle?"

"So, you did pick up a word or two. That was the best prank ever!" An impish grin stretched his face. "It was also the worst, because it was the only time I made my stepmother cry. I never did anything like that again."

Daci angled herself toward Jax as he continued telling tales on himself. From what she could tell, he'd been a handful, but a good kid where it counted. Like her own siblings. She found herself laughing and peppering him with questions.

"Losing your mom at an early age was very sad, but in so many ways you had a terrific childhood."

"I did." He nodded, but the smile fell off his face. "There was one other true childhood tragedy, though."

Daci gazed intently at his defined profile, noting the tension in his jaw and the slight hunch in his shoulders, as if he was curling in to protect himself.

"You don't have to tell me," she said.

"I want to, even though it's not something I talk about much. My dad and stepmom had another child, one that was biologically both of theirs, but..." Jax fell silent then cleared his throat. "My brother, Jason, was born with a congenital heart defect. No one knew about it until after he died in his sleep at six months old."

Reflexively, Daci's hand shot out and covered Jax's on the steering wheel. His muscles were tense, but he turned his palm and gave her fingers a brief squeeze.

"It's hard, you know, never getting to play with my little brother, tease him, fight with him and yet defend him from bullies on the playground. But it's comforting to be certain I will see him again, get to know him for all eternity."

Something like an arrow pierced Daci's chest, and a sob bubbled from her throat.

Jax shot her a sharp look. "I take it you don't know that for sure about your uncle."

"No, it's not that. I mean, yes, I have to admit I don't have a clue where my uncle stood with God, but that's not why your words hurt in such a good way."

"A good way?"

"Yes, it helped my faith to have someone say out loud what I've been thinking and hoping all along but not talking to anyone about." She told him about her brother born with FAS and then suddenly gone from her life without any proper opportunity to mourn.

Jax whistled through his teeth. "No wonder it's so hard for you with Serena and Chase. I admire you for sticking to it."

Daci smiled on the inside. Jax's approval— even admiration—meant more to her than she thought possible. How had she become so comfortable with him in these few days that long-held secrets of her heart came spilling out? It was a good thing she'd turned down his invitation to attend church with him. Even though, strangely, the idea had appealed to her, that's all she needed—people to start perceiving them as a couple. So not going to happen.

Jax clenched his jaw as he maintained a discreet distance between his car and Daci's, which cruised ahead of him one lane over. A few minutes ago, they had arrived back at the parking garage to collect his vehicle, where she had firmly declined his offer to follow her home and make sure there were no unpleasant surprises at her place. But her refusal hadn't been able to override his protective instinct. When he had been full-time in the Marshals Service, he'd been pretty good at tailing subjects without drawing their attention. This exercise would be a fair test to see if he'd maintained his skills.

What an awful day for Daci. She needed God more than she seemed to think she did. Too bad she wasn't open to attending church—at least not with him. Issuing the invitation hadn't been his brightest moment.

If he brought a woman to church, especially an attractive, age-appropriate one, the senior Ladies Aid contingent would start planning their wedding before the service was over. They were forever, bless their hearts, trying to set him up with a "nice girl." Apparently, at their ages of between sixty and eighty, any female under forty would qualify as a "girl." As for "nice," they were willing to give anyone a chance—but first the candidate would be subjected to an interrogation as thorough as any Fortune 500 company head-hunting a new CEO.

Jax shuddered. No, he didn't want to expose Daci to an ordeal like that. Maybe she'd find a church in her own neighborhood. Yes, that would be best.

Fifteen minutes later, Jax pulled his car over to the curb several houses away from Daci's and killed his headlights as she turned into her driveway and stopped beneath her carport. The entire street was empty—no foot or vehicle traffic. She lived in a quiet neighborhood, which was a good thing in that people who didn't belong would be noticed. And it was a bad thing in that folks hunkered down in their own houses at night. Cries for help might not be heard, and a careful intruder could escape detection.

Daci got out of her car and went into her duplex without a hitch. Apparently, no new gift baskets waited on her doorstep. A moment later, a light came on in the front room. Very shortly, that light went off and another glow showed through a heavy curtain in a room in the back corner, probably her bedroom.

Jax released a pent-up breath. She was indoors and settling in for the night. Still, he couldn't bring himself to put the car into gear and drive away. An all-night stakeout held no appeal, but neither did leaving Daci on her own when a killer was after her.

That business with her uncle had been as cold-blooded as murders came. Clinical. Professional. Not hot-blooded, which was the baffling aspect of this murder compared to the initial attempted hit-and-run on Daci, which smacked of impulsive rage or fear. The drive-by shooting had been definitely more planned, but gangsta style, lacking the intimacy and accuracy of the single bullet between Conrad Meyer's eyes. Meyer must have been looking straight into the face of his killer, maybe knew him…or her.

In its holder on the dash, the face of Jax's

cell phone lit up, and his ringtone began. He grinned. Daci. He activated the Bluetooth response.

"Hello."

"Go home." Her voice rang out firm and clear.

"You saw me?"

"No, but you're the protective type. Me telling you not to follow me home isn't going to stop you from doing it. I'm inside. I'm fine. All entrances are locked and bolted, and the security system is armed."

"Good to know. Thanks."

"Get some sleep. We'll talk tomorrow if you want to join me at the office to catch up on the status of the hunt for Naylor, as well as the search for the car involved in the near hit-and-run and the van involved in the drive-by shooting."

"Not to mention your plan of talking to DC Reynolds about tonight's events."

A groan carried across the airwaves. "Don't remind me. I don't want to contemplate that conversation any more tonight. He might be in since Naylor's still in the wind. If not, I'll have to call him."

"See you in the morning, then. I've had some thoughts we need to talk over."

"I can hardly wait." She let out a dry laugh.

"Now, let me get off the phone so I can call my siblings."

"You called *me*, remember?"

"Now I'm calling you *off*. Scram, Mr. Watchdog!"

"I'm on my way. Watch my lights cruise past your place."

Jax flipped on his headlights, put the car in gear and eased down on the accelerator. The curtain in the back room parted, and a shadowy figure waved as he went by. He waved back, even though she couldn't see him in the darkened car.

Making his way toward to his lonely, rather sterile warehouse reno near the river, an odd, fractured sensation grew inside of him—as if he'd left part of himself with Daci. Her kind of neighborhood was the sort of place where he'd lived when he was married and looking forward to raising a family. Afterward, he couldn't bear staying in the home he and Regan had bought together, so he sold it and moved deeper into the city. He didn't fit in with the trendy beehive of up-and-comers in his building, mostly younger than him, but he was hardly there except to sleep, and the location was close to work.

The next morning, he worked out at his health club for about an hour and then arrived at the US Marshals office around nine. Rey wasn't there, and Daci hadn't showed up yet. He occupied his waiting time catching up on reading reports.

Of all the reported Liggett Naylor sightings on which the Marshals Service had followed up, only one appeared credible. The escaped convict had stopped briefly to see a known associate in the Hyde Park neighborhood of Boston, which put him still in Massachusetts within the past twenty-four hours and specifically in Boston during the time period in which Conrad Meyer was killed. The proximity proved nothing, but it was an interesting coincidence. Or maybe not a coincidence. Perhaps they had been too quick to dismiss any connection with Naylor to Meyer's death, but what that connection might be remained a mystery. Another avenue to investigate.

The RAV4 that nearly ran him and Daci over in the street had not been identified or found. However, in a report transmitted to the Marshals Service from the Springfield PD, a rusty, bullet-riddled van matching the description of the one from the drive-by shooting had been discovered hunkered in the shade of an oak tree at the edge of a public park in Chicopee, a northern suburb of Springfield. The van had been wiped squeaky-clean of prints, which added an element of professionalism to what had looked like gang activity.

Jax frowned as he laid that report aside and glanced up at the wall clock. Nearly ten o'clock. Where was Daci? A chill coursed through him. He picked up his phone from Daci's desk, where he'd been waiting for her, and activated her number. The call went to voice mail. He grabbed his car keys and headed for the door.

"In case she's on the way here while I'm on the way there," he told the weekend duty clerk, "if Daci comes in, have her give me a call, would you?"

"Right!" The clerk shot him a wave.

Jax tried calling her again as he drove toward her place as quickly as he dared, but still got only voice mail. At last, her home came in view. He pulled to the curb, leaped out and dashed up to her door. All appeared peaceful and quiet, no sign of forced entry and no weird care packages on the porch, but none of that outward normalcy meant the occupant was okay. He thumbed the doorbell twice and waited, tapping his foot.

A giggle from his right drew his attention. A short, plump young woman waved at him from the porch of the house next door.

She turned away and motioned toward

someone. "Daci, you've got company, and he's cu-u-u-ute."

"Oh, no!" Daci's exclamation reached him from the opposite porch and then her trim figure appeared at the rail. "I'm so sorry, Jax. I was over here meeting Jewel's sister and baby niece and lost track of time."

His knees went weak at seeing her safe with her luxurious strawberry blond hair loose and cascading around her shoulders. She was dressed in blue jeans and a T-shirt and wore a welcoming, if apologetic, smile on her face. He inhaled a deep breath and willed his heart rate to slow down to normal. The rebellious organ had been trying to jump out of his chest, though whether that reaction was from relief or the involuntary surge of attraction for her he didn't care to decipher.

"I'm just glad you're okay," he said. Did his voice sound as breathless as he felt?

"Come over and meet my new friends."

Jax joined the small group on the neighboring porch, and Daci introduced him to Jewel, Cherise and Mandy, three of the residents at the group home, as well as Tanisha Grey, one of the caregivers. Before Daci could get to her, Jewel's sister stuck out her hand and introduced herself and the baby, who slept on even as she was passed from one person to another.

"There are six young women living here," Daci said. "But Hannah and Allie have part-time jobs and are working today. Paige is in the house. She hasn't really warmed up to me yet."

Cherise sniffed. "Paige doesn't say much to us, either, but she is always on the computer talking to some guy from her church's Uniquely Made group."

"Uniquely Made?" Jax looked from one to another, seeking an explanation.

Tanisha laughed. "One of the local churches has a Bible study and activity group especially for adults born with extra challenges in their mental, emotional or social development."

Daci's face lit up. "That sounds like a wonderful program."

Jax's heart leaped. Daci sounded really interested. Maybe she would be drawn to attend that church and get reconnected to the faith her grandmother had tried to instill in her.

Mandy lifted a hand. "I go there, too. I'm a Down's girl, and I'm special."

The innocence of her beaming smile and matter-of-fact statement warmed Jax to his socks. He could understand why Daci had been drawn to come over here and visit, especially when she was going through a stressful time.

They chatted for a while, and then Daci headed for the porch steps. "See you later, ladies. We should probably get going, Jax—now that I've wasted half our morning." She wrinkled her nose at him, a terminally cute mannerism that affected him more than he liked.

Jax fell into step with her as they crossed the lawn toward her place. "I tried calling, but got no answer, so raced over here like my tail was on fire."

"I really am sorry. I should have at least texted you when it appeared I wouldn't get to the office as soon as I'd intended. Left my phone on the charger when I stepped outside to retrieve the newspaper, and then the girls here waved me over, and one thing led to another."

"No worries. I officially forgive you for scaring a decade off my life."

"And I officially thank you for caring enough to check on me. It's a weird feeling to have someone looking out after me. I'm such an independent character that I'm surprised I like it."

They paused at the bottom of her porch steps, and she gazed up at him with those deep brown eyes. Her sincerity and humility all but undid him. If this were a date, he'd kiss her right now—despite the audience next door.

Instead, he stuffed his hands into his pockets. "That's what partners are for."

"Right. Partners." Her gaze went shuttered

even as she turned and led the way up her steps. "Come in while I morph into a deputy marshal."

He followed her inside and found himself in a living room furnished with simple but quality pieces and a color scheme of rich cream accented by browns and blues. Nothing about the decor suggested excessive wealth, just good taste. But then a hint of the same sterility of his own place struck him. Except for some photographs on the fireplace mantel, very little of a personal nature graced the space, but perhaps that was because she hadn't lived here long.

Daci retired to the back room while he gravitated toward the photos. The same people were featured in all of them, but at varying ages. Most were casual shots involving a pair of look-alike young males and two females who resembled each other but weren't identical. He could pick out the family relationship in all of them, mostly through the eyes, which were all deep brown, and the noses, all straight and elegant, and the chins, firm and round. The face of a fifth person, an older woman with the same telltale features, filled the central frame of the grouping. The eyes were tired, but the face was serene, perhaps a little stoic. Photos of Daci's parents were noticeably absent.

"These are your siblings and your grand-mother?" he called to her.

"Good eye, Sherlock," she called back with a laugh. "Grab yourself a drink from the fridge if you want. I'll be a few more minutes."

Jax checked out the refrigerator and found it considerably more stocked than his own. She must actually cook once in a while. He selected a can of iced tea and popped the tab. The container was only half empty when she rejoined him, looking like the tightly put together Daci he'd first met. Inwardly, he mourned the reappearance of that bun at the base of her neck.

"Did you get in touch with your sisters and brothers last night?"

She nodded, a frown tugging at the corners of her lips. "They were shocked, as I predicted, but Nate maybe less so."

"How do you mean?"

"He told me Uncle Con called him a couple of days ago. As if the phone call itself wasn't enough of a surprise, instead of his usual gloomy attitude he apparently sounded almost jolly, but with an anxious, sort of manic edge. The last thing he said to my brother was 'tell your mamasis to look after herself.' Nate felt like the comment was off-key with the tone of the rest of the conversation, but wrote it off to Con's awkward social skills and forgot about it."

Jax frowned and crossed his arms. "Have you told your siblings about the attempts on your life?"

"So far, just Nate. I had to come clean after he shared that strange conversation with me."

"I think you should—"

A special ringtone from his phone cut off his sentence. He answered immediately. Tiny prickles cascaded over his skin as the Marshals Service desk clerk spoke.

He ended the call and met Daci's expectant stare. "The PD just pulled a red RAV4 out of the Connecticut River. There's a body in it."

SIX

With Jax a strong presence at her back, Daci stood in the thick of the activity at the vehi-cle-recovery scene. Clouds boiled in from the west, veiling the sun, and the wind kicked up angry-looking waves in the blue-gray water of the Connecticut River. The rumble of distant thunder promised rain.

A shiver shook Daci's body—not because of the impending squall, but from the face of the dead man who lay limp on a tarp at her feet. A bullet hole in the man's forehead was identical to Conrad's wound, but even that gruesome detail was not what had frozen her insides into a massive block of ice. The weight of her shocked, horrified recognition nearly doubled her over.

"I know him." The words sprang from her lips in a ragged whisper.

"I do, too," Jax said. "He's the owner of

Sam's Clams, that restaurant we almost went to on the day we met."

"Restaurant owner!" Daci jerked. "Are you kidding? How can that be?" Hot emotions stormed through her, shattering the ice and turning the shivers to quakes she was helpless to stop.

Jax grabbed her elbow and turned her to face him. "What's wrong, Daci?"

"This man," she spit out, pointing a quivering finger toward the dead body, "shot my grandmother!"

Jax's mouth fell open, but no words came out. Daci wrenched away from him and stalked toward her department car. Within a few steps, her legs turned to jelly and she crumpled to her knees. Hot tears cut paths down her cheeks even as cold raindrops began to pelt her face. She hugged herself tightly to bottle the sobs.

She was making a complete fool of herself in front of fellow law-enforcement officers, including Detective Herriman, who was in charge of the investigation and standing nearby. If his eyes were on her, he must be marking her down as a hysteric unable to hack the rigors of the job.

A moment later, a clean-cut face swam into cloudy view and a pair of warm hands gripped hers. Jax had knelt in front of her.

"You're sure?" he queried gently.

"His face is engraved in my brain!" She hauled in a deep breath and let it out slowly. "He's aged fourteen years, but I recognize him."

"I believe you. This information is important to the case. We need to talk with Herriman, but not here. Downtown. Out of the rain. Head for the car, and I'll let him know we need to meet when he's done here."

Nodding dumbly, Daci allowed him to help her to her feet. Good thing the two of them were not alone, or she might give in to the temptation to melt into the comfort of his embrace. She was starting to depend too much on this guy. She needed to watch herself.

Stuffing her hands into her pockets, she marched to the unmarked sedan and climbed into the passenger seat. Jax soon joined her, assuming the driver's seat without comment. As they drove to the police station, she watched the windshield stream with what looked like the buckets of tears yet lurking behind her eyes.

"How did a carjacker and murderer become a respected business owner?" She released a pent-up question—one of the least volatile among those scrambling around in her brain.

"I would guess on the profits from carjacking."

"But crooks don't readily turn from the easy dime to hard work. The restaurant business is tough."

"Maybe killing your grandmother scared him straight."

Daci's heart lightened the barest fraction. "Grandma would have liked that. But even if he changed, it apparently was not enough to resist attempting to kill again when he saw me in the street."

"You're guessing a moment of horrified recognition led to a panic reaction?"

"Excellent description. You are most definitely a wordsmith."

"Handy trait in a lawyer...or a used-car salesman."

"You said it." If Daci could have smiled, she would have. How she enjoyed their banter. "I'm thinking more along the lines that he caught a glimpse of me when I ate at his restaurant last week, has been fretting himself into a frenzy over my presence in his neighborhood. Then when he saw me in the street, he reacted on impulse."

Jax gave a soft hum. "Plausible. Then what? He hired some gang members to finish the job he failed?"

"Maybe, but I don't want to connect too

many dots too quickly. Something more is going on here."

"Agreed. Did the person who killed your uncle also kill the guy who killed your grandma and tried to kill you? If so, what is the connection?"

Minutes later, they sat across from Herriman in front of his desk, nursing typically horrible cop-shop coffee. Daci grimaced at the scummy blackness, but at least the sludge provided warmth in her belly.

For Herriman, Jax laid out the facts about her uncle's death and the similarity in the execution-style killings between his murder and that of the driver of the RAV4. Daci added her recognition of the man as the carjacker who killed her grandmother, grateful that her voice emerged steady and professional after the emotional tsunami that had overwhelmed her at the river. Herriman's gaze conveyed no judgment about that embarrassing moment. Maybe he hadn't noticed her meltdown. Not likely, but she could hope.

The detective nodded. "The ID on the RAV4 guy says his name was Samuel Clayhorn. He was the owner of—"

"Sam's Clams," Jax finished for him.

"You know him?"

"Only by sight from eating at the restaurant. Didn't know his name until now."

Herriman tapped on his computer. "What do you know? Sammy-boy has a sheet. Petty theft, minor graft mostly. Got sent up for a year at Mass Correctional when he was twenty years old. Released on probation eight months later, but started hanging out with a bad crowd again. Notes here says the probation officer was nervous that Sam was getting close to breaking the conditions of his parole when the guy suddenly turned choirboy. Clean as a whistle until now."

"Fits," Daci said. "He looked late teens or early twenties when he killed my grandmother."

Jax frowned. "For a petty grifter to suddenly turn carjacker and murderer, that 'bad crowd' must have included someone with the kind of connections to handle a stolen vehicle of Lexus caliber."

Herriman leaned forward, elbows on his desk. "Believe me, as part of the investigation, we'll be taking a very close look at this guy's business."

"You think the restaurant might be a front for something crooked?" Jax's question sounded speculative rather than inquiring.

"If it's a front for money laundering or something of that nature," Daci said, "it would be doubly important to eliminate someone like me who could connect him to a crime that has no statute of limitations. He couldn't afford for his past to catch up with him. Whoever he's answerable to would be seriously displeased."

"True." Herriman nodded. "Plus, he'd spend the rest of his natural life behind bars."

"So, I get the incentive to kill me, but why is he the one who is dead?"

Jax shot her a sidelong look. "I would say that's one of many important details we don't have nailed down yet."

Daci's stomach churned. "I have a more disturbing question. If Sam Clayhorn has a record, why did I not find his mug shot in the photos the police had me poring over for days after the tragedy?"

A frown etched deep lines in the detective's face. "Let me look into what was going on in the force at that time and dig deeper into Clayhorn. There must have been a reason for the exclusion. I'll connect with the PD in Boston, too. See if there are other commonalities between the two recent murders."

"Keep us informed." Jax rose, and Daci followed suit.

They shook hands with the detective and headed for the vehicle. The rain had passed, and the partly cloudy sky allowed sunlight to peek through, warming the air.

Daci's spirits lifted. With the man who had killed her grandmother identified and no longer a threat to her or her family, she might begin to find closure on that horrible incident from her past. Who had killed Clayhorn, and if the murder of her uncle might be connected, remained to be discovered, but as for this moment, the man who had been trying to kill her was dead, which meant there was no reason she would need to be taken off the Naylor case. Why not do something proactive to fulfill her duties?

"You up for some lunch?" Jax asked, tossing the car keys in the air and catching them.

On the next toss, Daci snatched them. "I am, but not with you." She laughed at his crestfallen expression. "Not today anyway."

They stopped beside the sedan. "My assignment is to cozy up to Serena Farnam. I think I'm going to invite her out for lunch. Naylor was last seen in Boston. I'm going to finesse what I can out of her about places her ex might hide in that city. The woman knows something. I'm sure of it. But she may not realize what she knows."

Jax chuckled. "If anyone can finesse her, my vote is with you."

"Thanks, partner." She grinned back at him.

An hour later, she'd dropped Jax off outside her place to collect his vehicle and then she met Serena at a Mexican restaurant the young woman favored. Serena had been over the moon that someone was interested in spending time with her.

"You and me," she said. "We click, you know, right?"

Daci smiled, guilt smiting her. This undercover work could be heart-wrenching. "We have important things in common—like our love for babies and our commitment to protect Chase."

"You got that right, sista." Serena began studying the menu.

Daci's mouth watered. Odors of peppers and onions and sizzling meat wafted around her. She took a homemade tortilla chip from the basket between them, scooped up some salsa and popped it into her mouth. The flavors exploded on her tongue, and an appreciative moan left her throat.

"Great eats, huh?" Serena grinned. "I'm having beef fajitas."

"I think I'll go for the chimichangas."

After they ordered, Daci leaned across the table toward the younger woman. "Speaking of keeping the little guy safe, any sign of you-know-who?"

Shadows clouded Serena's gaze. "No, and I wish he'd be caught. Worrying he might go after my boy again is… Well, it's like trying to breathe but getting no air. Sometimes I can hardly stand it. You know? I want to be with him 24/7. Protect him. Do you get that?"

"Totally." Daci cocked her head. "Will you see Chase over the weekend?"

Serena's face went radiant. "This afternoon. I get a supervised visit at the park."

"Great! Mind if I tag along? I've got nothing else to do today."

The younger woman shrugged. "Why not? With another person there, maybe the social services worker won't hover over us like I might do a runner. I'd be super tempted to do it if I thought it would get us safe from my ex."

A cunning expression flitted across her face—there and gone so fast not many would have caught it. Did Serena have an escape plan percolating in the back of her mind?

"You don't have anywhere safe to go?" Daci asked. "What about asking the police for protective custody?"

Serena snorted. "Too many dirty cops. Liggey always bragged he had the system in his pocket."

"But you don't know who the dirty ones are."

The younger woman rolled a shoulder. "If he ever mentioned a name, I was too sloshed to remember." She wrinkled her forehead. "He did like to laugh about having 'it' on a leash."

"It? Not a person?"

Serena spread her hands that sported newly shortened but still brightly colored nails. "Never knew what he meant, but he thought it was a big joke."

Their food came, and Daci left the subject rather than arouse Serena's suspicions about her motives. They could talk more when they got together with Chase. Besides, the intense flavor of the Mexican cuisine commanded her full attention.

After the meal, Daci followed Serena to a nearby park dotted with trees and lined with footpaths. Daci pulled in next to Serena's rusty Chevrolet. Glancing over at the younger woman's vehicle, Daci's eyebrows lifted. The infant seat in the rear of the car spoke volumes about the hope Serena held for reclaiming custody of her son.

Nodding approval of the proactive preparations, Daci grabbed her purse—heavier than usual with the bulk of her service pistol—and got out of her VW. Her gaze scanned the area. A few joggers were in view on the paths, and a trio of mothers watched small children play on equipment about fifty yards distant. To her left, a picnic shelter was vacant, but on her right, sunlight glinted off gazing globes mounted on pedestals that flanked a bench. A man dressed in chinos and a light jacket over a polo shirt occupied the seat. He was rolling a stroller back and forth in front of him while the occupant slept.

"Jaxton Williams!" Serena planted her fists on her hips. "What are you doing here with my son?"

Good question. Daci wanted to know the same thing. She also wanted to know what right a knock-'em-dead suit-and-tie guy had to look so good in casual attire, also.

Jax smiled innocently, shooting Daci a pointed glance over Serena's shoulder. "The social services worker had something come up, so I'm filling in today."

Daci smirked. Right! Something came up—like Jax calling to ask if he could substitute for the regular worker. Great thinking, though he couldn't have known for certain that she would accompany Serena here after lunch. Now Serena and Chase were double covered by their presence. Triple, actually, since surveillance never left either of the subjects. In a vehicle somewhere inconspicuous a duo of PD officers or deputy marshals would be watching them. Boring stuff but necessary.

The baby suddenly awakened with a cry. A pacifier flew out of the stroller and landed at the base of one of the gazing globe pedestals. Grinning, Daci bent to retrieve the article. The pacifier would have to be wiped with antiseptic.

Above her lowered head, the gazing globe suddenly exploded, showering her hair with glass. A thunderclap instantly followed.

Daci's heart rate plunged into overdrive.

Not a thunderclap. The report of a rifle aimed at *her*!

Shock-paralysis passed in an instant, and Jax lunged toward the women and the infant's stroller, herding them behind the meager cover of the bench. As they crouched there, Serena found her voice and began to scream, which agitated Chase into wailing and kicking. Daci—showing the cool head he'd come to expect from her—was immediately on her phone, calling for help.

Jax pulled his pistol from his armpit holster, thankful that he'd listened to his protective instincts and strapped it on for this meeting. He ventured a peek around one of the gazing globe pedestals. No rifle shot greeted him, and no one was in view in the direction where the initial shot had originated.

Had the shooter taken off after the failed assassination attempt, or was he angling around behind trees and bushes, trying to get another bead on his target? On Daci.

Why was Daci still in danger when the man who'd tried to run her over and probably hired the drive-by shooters lay on a slab in the morgue? Clearly, they were missing critical information that would answer that question.

Jax glanced over his shoulder toward the women and picked up a flash of sunlight on metal from a set of distant bushes.

"Look out!" He tackled Daci flat onto her back as another shot rang out. A fist-sized hole opened in the back of the wooden bench, spraying all of them with splinters. Fresh screams came from the playground area. Hopefully, those mothers were gathering up their children and vacating the area, but he couldn't turn around to check.

God, help us all!

"Get off!" Daci shoved at him.

Jax rolled over into a crouch and fired a shot toward the distant bushes. It was a futile move, pistol against long-range rifle, but he had to do something, if only to let the shooter know he wasn't the only one armed.

A sharp smack of palm against flesh abruptly morphed Serena's screams into whimpers. Daci was taking charge of the hysteria.

"Go, girl!" Daci's voice commanded. "Get Chase back to his foster home. Drive away and don't look back. It's me they're after."

Jax gritted his teeth. The surveillance team was likely closing in on the situation right now. Hopefully, they'd intercept Serena and Chase and escort them to safety. Their presence would now be exposed, but there was no help for it in this situation.

Serena's fading sobs and the rattle of the stroller moving away at high speed alerted Jax to the young woman's obedience to Daci's instructions. His heart lightened marginally. The fewer people in the line of fire the better.

He twisted and grasped Daci's arm. "Let's go for the picnic shelter before he gets you in his sights again."

Without a word, Daci pulled her own pistol from her purse and took off, zigzagging in a crouching lope as they'd been trained to do. Jax followed, weaving a different trajectory toward the same location.

Crack! The shot reverberated through the park.

Daci stumbled and dropped her gun. Jax's heart leaped into his throat. He closed the distance between them as she righted herself and staggered onward, minus her pistol. Throwing an arm around her slender waist, he half carried her into the shelter. A stone fireplace surround jutted from the far wall. He shoved her against it and took a position facing outward in front of her, sweeping his gun and his gaze from side to side.

"Come on, you coward," he muttered. "Show yourself."

A pair of gunshots sounded from the direction where the shooter had been crouching. The distinctive sounds indicated pistols, not a rifle. The surveillance team assigned to Serena must be getting in on the action. Probably they hadn't been near enough to the scene to intercept Serena and Chase, but were providing cover for her getaway. Hopefully, they'd take the sniper out or at least drive him away.

The shrill of sirens began closing in on their location. Soon, the area swarmed with uniformed officers and an armed-to-the-teeth SWAT team. Jax hollered for medical help.

He turned toward Daci and caught her as she slid down the wall, leaving a red trail on the stone. "Where are you hit?"

She seemed to struggle to focus on his face. "Feels like a hive of hornets have taken up residence in my right side."

The words came out slurred. Jax yelled again for the medical team. A moment later, he was pulled away from her to make room for a pair of EMTs.

Time that had crawled during the minutes when they were under fire seemed to speed into overdrive as many things happened at once. A plainclothes detective, not Herriman, was in his face even as he tried to monitor what was happening with Daci. He gave his terse account of events while she was tended and loaded onto a gurney. Her eyes were closed in a ghastly pale face, and she lay unnaturally still.

Jax's lungs constricted. *Please, Lord, pull her through!*

The medical team began wheeling her toward the waiting ambulance, and Jax took a step in that direction. A big hand closed around his biceps, halting his progress. He whirled on the person who was attempting to keep him from Daci's side and came face-to-face with DC Reynolds. Of course, their boss been called in.

"She's in good hands," Rey said. "If you want to protect her, we've got to get to the bottom of who is after her and stop him."

Jax's shoulders wilted. "I know."

Rey's eyes narrowed. "You're not falling for her, are you?"

"Get real! She's in law enforcement. I can't! You know that better than anyone."

His old partner's face folded into grim lines. "I remember, but attraction has amnesia."

A change of subject was in order. "Did Daci call you yet about the murder of her uncle last night in Boston?"

Rey's eyes narrowed and his jaw tensed.

"Clearly not. We were sidetracked by another dead body this morning." Jax's gaze followed the ambulance as it tore out of the parking lot, lights and siren activated. "I need to head for the hospital."

"Let's go together," Rey said. "Ride with me, and I'll have someone bring your car over later. You can fill me in about Daci's uncle on the way."

Jax didn't argue. Anything to get to the hospital pronto.

There was so much to tell, including a discussion about Daci's recognition of the murdered man in the RAV4, that he and Rey had scarcely finished going over the basics when they arrived in the hospital parking lot. Jax jumped out of the car and hustled inside.

At the registration desk, Rey caught up with him, and they were directed to the surgical floor, where Daci had been taken. The nurses at the floor desk could tell them nothing except that Daci was alive and in surgery. Prognosis wasn't on the radar yet. Nor did the charge nurse have any idea how long the surgery would take.

Jax's gut churned as he and Rey entered the waiting room. He had no interest in sitting down. He turned toward his boss, who hovered in the doorway as if about to leave.

"You'll be stationing a guard at her door, right?"

"You know it. The deputy who is bringing your car will stand first watch. Since the Naylor sighting in Boston, the hunt is mostly going forward from that office, so I'll be able reassign a couple of Springfield deputies to dig into these attempts on Daci."

"Sounds good. Could I be one of those reassigned deputies? I think I'll go nuts if I have to sit and do nothing for who knows how long. Turn me loose to follow up on some leads."

"No can do." The other man shook his head. "The Marshals Service brought you on for the Naylor case in a narrow capacity where that case intersected with Serena and Chase's well-being. While we were speculating that the attempts on Daci might be Naylor trying eliminate an obstacle between him and Serena and his son, I gave you latitude to investigate. But I can see no reason to go on thinking that Naylor has any connection with the attempts on deputy marshal Candace Marlowe's life. It makes more sense to believe the perp is the same as the one who murdered Conrad Meyer and Samuel Clayhorn. Sorry, but that takes you out of the equation." Rey put a hand on Jax's arm. "Let us do our job. We're good at it."

"So was I. C'mon, Rey! One of our own as been shot."

"*Our* own? Listen to yourself, Jax. Don't get sucked into this life again. It's not what you want. Hang tough. I *will* keep you informed." He smacked a palm against the doorjamb, jerked a nod and walked away.

Staring after him, Jax furled and unfurled his fists at his sides. Frustration didn't begin to describe this moment. He was *not* sitting around a hospital waiting room, tapping his toes and twiddling his thumbs. So, he was relegated to matters involving Serena and Chase, was he? Well, then, he would go talk to her. Reassuring himself of her and Chase's well-being offered a plausible reason to interview her as a witness to today's incident.

Jax went to the nurses' desk, explained that he was Daci's partner and left his card with instructions to call him when she got out of surgery. Heading for the elevator, he found a uniformed deputy coming toward him, holding out his car keys. A new guy he didn't recognize from his days with the Marshals Service.

"It's in the main lot," the deputy said.

"Good timing," Jax told the man. "Take good care of Daci, now, will you?"

"That's for certain." The deputy nodded and headed onward toward the nurses' desk.

In his car, Jax got on the phone to Chase's foster parents, where Serena was supposed to have taken him. No, they told him, she and the baby hadn't shown up yet. The corkscrew in his gut wound tighter.

"Serena, what are you pulling now?" he muttered under his breath and tapped her number.

The phone call went to voice mail. He left a terse message to call him back ASAP. People were worried about her.

Driving toward Serena's apartment building as fast as he dared, he activated his Bluetooth and called Rey. At least it was Saturday, so traffic was lighter than on a workday.

"Reynolds," the DC answered the call.

"Serena hasn't delivered Chase to his foster parents, and she's not answering her phone. I'm on my way to her apartment now."

Rey mumbled an angry word. "Her surveillance team is still debriefing about the shoot-

5

5

Jill Elizabeth Nelson

ing at the park. I'll send someone to meet you at Serena's and put out an APB on her vehicle."

"Thanks." Jax ended the call.

Fifteen minutes later, he pounded on the cracked and peeling door of Serena's apartment. Odors of stale grease and dilapidation assailed him, and thin walls made him privy to an argument going on in the apartment next door.

One of the goals before uniting Serena with her son was to get them into better housing, but if she had taken off with her baby for parts unknown, once the authorities caught up with her she might permanently lose her chance at custody. Very sad, but he preferred that scenario to the prospect that Serena and Chase might have been taken by thugs in Naylor's employ.

Jax pounded on the door again. No response. Silence from within.

At the sound of footsteps approaching up the hall, he turned. It was Steve Green, one of the deputies he'd worked with several years back. The guy was as linebacker husky as ever.

"Good to see a familiar face," Jax said. "Serena either isn't here or isn't answering the door."

"In light of the shooting incident, we can make a case for probable cause to suspect foul play and enter forcibly."

"That's what I like to hear." He sent the man a shark grin.

Green scanned the door up and down. "Shouldn't be too difficult to pop this one."

He gave it a flat-footed kick with a booted foot. The door popped open and slapped the wall with a soft bang. Jax rushed in, pistol at the ready. The place might be shabby and small, but at least Serena was keeping it neat and clean, according to the requirements of her rehabilitation plan. However, neither she nor Chase were in evidence as Jax and Green searched through the bedroom, bathroom, and postage-stamp kitchen.

Jax holstered his gun. "I don't think she's been here."

"Which means she's in the wind." Green pulled out his phone. "I'll let the DC know."

Jax's cell sounded, and he walked into the hallway, tugging it from his shirt pocket. Not a number he recognized. Could be the hospital. His heart leaped. *Please, God, let it be good news.*

"Williams," he said.

"Mr. Williams," answered a pleasant female voice, "Ms. Candace Marlowe is under medical supervision in the recovery area now. She's stable and should be ready to be transferred to a private room in about an hour."

A buoyant sensation filled his chest. Daci had made it through the surgery! "Thank you for calling."

He could hug someone, but Deputy Green might find that expression of emotion a little over-the-top.

Had anyone notified her siblings she'd been shot? He didn't have their numbers. They'd be in Daci's phone. When he went back to the hospital, if she was conscious he'd ask her permission to use her phone to give them a call. She'd been balky about telling them of the threats to her life so the news might come as an abrupt shock, but it had to be done.

Green joined him in the hallway. "DC's pulling in full staff to work on finding Serena and Chase because of their connection to Naylor. All roads out of Springfield, but especially toward Boston, are being watched. If his goons are taking them to him, and we can follow, we might nab him. Protection for Daci is being handed over to the PD as of this minute. Hospital security has agreed to look after her until an officer can get there."

Jax ground his teeth together. Not that the police department wasn't fully competent, but it went against the grain for the Marshals Service not to spare a deputy to protect one of their own.

"I guess I'll return to the hospital, then. They just called to say she's out of surgery."

"Good news!" Green smiled. "But the boss said to ask if you know anyone Serena might turn to if she was doing a runner or being pursued."

"I have a list of Serena's known friends and associates on my office computer. I can stop there on my way and email it to the duty clerk for dissemination."

"Great! Thanks."

They headed to their separate vehicles.

Driving to his law office, Jax prayed for Serena and Chase's safety. How did situations get to be such a mess with all questions and no answers?

After performing his task for the Marshals Service, he arrived back at the hospital a little over an hour since they'd called him. She might be in her own room by now. The front desk confirmed her transfer and said she'd only just arrived in that room.

Jax smiled and hurried along. His might be the first familiar face at her bedside. He would have it no other way. How pathetic was that desire for a guy who didn't dare allow their relationship to continue past this case? The mental scolding had no power to slow him down.

"Hold on, Williams."

Jax turned. Tim Baker, a PD uniform known to him from his work as an attorney, was speed-walking after him.

"I'm taking first shift on Deputy Marlowe's protection detail." Baker fell into step with Jax. "Heard you were there for the gun battle."

"Not much of a battle. Pistol against rifle was a poor contest, but backup was quick to get there, and somehow we managed to stay alive."

They reached Daci's floor, but with hallways heading in different confusing directions, Jax asked the way to her room number.

"Up that way." The nurse pointed.

"Thanks," Baker said. "I'll go relieve hospital security on her guard detail now."

"Hospital security?" The nurse's brows drew together. "I don't think so. That nice deputy marshal's been hovering around waiting for her arrival on this floor. He's maybe half a minute ahead of you."

Jax's heart stopped and then plunged into a gallop. Whirling, he took off up the hallway, Baker's shout and footsteps following on his heels.

With all deputies in the field, if one was here, he had to be an impostor. Personnel, patients and equipment blocked his way, but he dodged and wove with the single-minded determination of a football running back with the goal line in sight.

Where *was* that room? There!

He barreled through the door into hazy dimness. Someone had shut off the light. Jax flipped it on, and his blood went arctic. The man in a Marshals Service uniform who had brought him his car keys leaned over Daci's bed, jamming a pillow into her face.

SEVEN

Through a mental fog, Daci fought for breath. Something dense but fluffy molded itself to her face, obstructing her nose and mouth. If only she could move—fight! But the commands from her mind didn't seem to reach her limbs. Her arms remained at her sides. Something seemed to bind them in place.

She heaved with her midsection. Pain screamed through every pore and out her mouth, releasing the last vestiges of much-needed oxygen.

Someone shouted. A familiar voice—one that made her feel safer in spite of her fear.

Footsteps pounded. The obstruction over her face eased, but did not disappear. A metallic crash assaulted her ears, and she flinched. Human grunts and the smacks of fists on flesh filled the air. A marginal amount of oxygen reached her lungs, and her mind cleared the smallest bit. She willed her arms to move, but they yanked uselessly against restraints.

Where was she? What was going on?

She turned her head to the side, away from the object covering her face, and more oxygen filled her lungs. Of course! She'd been shot and was in the hospital. But why were her arms tied to the guardrails of the bed, and who had put this pillow over her face? More to the point, who was fighting with the person who had tried to asphyxiate her?

Jax!

Yes, that was the voice she'd heard shouting.

"Freeze!" A different voice hollered. "Hold it right there!"

The hand-to-hand battle went silent, and a third voice started cursing as the familiar click of handcuffs met Daci's ears. A moment later, the pillow was stripped from her face, and Daci blinked up at a most welcome sight—Jax's face. The right side of his bottom lip was split and puffy, and a trickle of blood had cut a path from there to his chin, but he was beautiful.

"Jax." She breathed his name. "Thank you."

"You're welcome." He undid the strips of cloth holding her wrists to the bed's side rails. "Creep must have tied you up so you couldn't fight even if you awakened. Are you all right?"

"I—I think so." She raised a hand to brush hair from her face. The movement hurt. "My side feels like a hot poker is stirring up coals in there."

The uninjured half of his mouth tilted upward. "A few hours ago, it was a hornet's nest. Now it's coals and a hot poker? What next—a branding iron?"

A snicker escaped her lungs, drawing a fresh pang from her side. "Don't make me laugh. It hurts too much."

A man in PD uniform began giving the Miranda warning to the prisoner. Daci's gaze moved to the sullen captive. He was a stocky Hispanic of medium height and bland features. Probably midthirties. Not anyone's idea of a cold-blooded killer, but his actions proved that he was certainly that. And hc was posing as a deputy marshal.

Daci lifted her head, despite the twinge of pain, and gasped at the mess in her room where the bedside table and all of its contents had flown every which way.

She glared at the imposter. "Who are you, and where did you get that uniform?"

The bland face turned wicked in a sneer, but he said nothing.

A hospital security guard burst into the room, pistol at the ready. "Nobody move!" In a shooter's crouch, he stared from the two men in uniform to Daci with Jax at her bedside. "What's going on in here?"

Daci pointed toward her attacker. "That man tried to suffocate me."

The guard's gaze narrowed on the PD officer and the man in the deputy marshal's uniform standing next to each other. "Which one?" he asked.

The words *the one who shouldn't be in that uniform* almost left her lips, but her brain, still a bit muddled from the aftereffects of anesthesia, corrected itself in the nick of time. "The one in handcuffs."

"Oh." The guard lowered his pistol.

"Everything is under control now," the officer said. "This man is under arrest for attempted murder and impersonating a United States Deputy Marshal."

"Get medical staff in here, please," Jax added. "Daci's had a horrible shock on top of surgery. I hope she hasn't torn her wound open."

"I can do that." The guard holstered his gun and left.

"Baker," Jax said, "search this guy's pocket for keys and then find his car. It's possible he stole the uniform from the real deputy who brought my vehicle from the shooting scene at the park."

The men exchanged grim gazes. Daci's lungs constricted. Who knew what this killer had done to the other deputy in order to get his uniform? Had the vendetta against her cost a colleague his life?

"Will do." The officer Jax had referred to as Baker jerked a nod and shoved the suspect toward the door.

"Wait!" Weariness like a heavy tide flowed through Daci, but she forced herself onto one elbow.

Jax gripped her arm. "Relax. You're safe."

She met his deep blue gaze. "There will be no relaxation or safety until we get to the bottom of who wants me dead and why." Her jaw tensed as she turned her stare on her attacker. "Any answers for me?"

The man chuckled. Not a pleasant sound. "A big price has been placed on your head, *chica*, and I'm not the only one eager to collect it."

"Why the bounty?" Jax barked.

The would-be assassin shrugged thick shoulders. "Nobody knows. Nobody cares, as long as the pay is good."

With a deep groan, Daci settled back onto her bed, barely aware of Officer Baker and the attacker leaving the room. Her reading of the man's body language said he wasn't lying. The guy really didn't know why she was being targeted and truly didn't care. They were no closer to finding out who wanted to plant her six feet under or why her death was worth so much to that person.

A nurse and a doctor hustled in. The nurse fussed at Jax to leave the room, but he wasn't accepting any shooing away. Daci said it was okay for him to remain, and the tension eased. The doctor, a woman with a Middle Eastern complexion, checked her sutures— holding fine—took her vital signs, including air saturation, and pronounced her no worse for the wear. The nurse offered pain medication, which Daci gladly accepted, and then said she'd have housekeeping come in to clean up the mess. She uttered that last sentence as she left the room with a glare toward Jax, who stood stoically near the far wall with his arms crossed.

Daci managed a faint grin at the territorial byplay, then turned her attention toward the doctor. "What's the damage, and what is my prognosis?"

The woman bestowed a patient, though weary, smile. "As you know, you sustained a gunshot wound to the right flank. The bullet entered here." She pointed to her lower right side nearer the back than the front. "And exited here." She moved her finger toward the edge of her waistline. "You can be thankful that most of the damage was to muscle and tissue. Only the slightest invasion into the abdominal cavity occurred. Deeper penetration would have been catastrophic. We stopped the hemorrhaging from a nicked blood vessel and repaired the tissue damage, but you are going to be quite sore in your abdominal region for a number of weeks. The soft organs in your abdomen were bruised from being tossed around by the velocity of the bullet passing through, and they will need significant time to recover."

"How long can she be kept in the hospital?" Jax asked.

"How soon can I get out?" Daci amended.

The doctor looked from one to the other, dark brows arched. "I would not like to discharge you before we are certain all internal bleeding has been addressed and also that the swelling in the bruised organs is diminishing and they are functioning properly. Plus, we must closely monitor you for infection. Four or five days, I would think."

"Three days," Daci said firmly.

The doctor's brown eyes twinkled. "You are determined, and mental attitude helps with healing, but too much activity too soon will set you back and lengthen your recovery time. Even when you are released to go home, you will need to take it quite easy for a month or so. But we can discuss those parameters later." The woman patted Daci's hand. She glanced at Jax then back to Daci, brow furrowed. "Is it safe to leave you now?"

"She'll be fine with me." Jax stepped forward.

Daci nodded. Of course, she *would* be safe with him physically, but emotionally not so much. Just looking at him standing there, wearing blood on his face that he'd spilled in her defense, turned her heart to mush. When had anyone except her grandmother ever looked after *her* instead of the other way around?

She closed her eyes. As if she could resist any longer the pull of morphine in her system! It was tempting to fight to stay awake, but her body required rest. She had to get her strength back. She was going to need it. Weeks of taking it easy? Not going to happen. In fact, a plan was forming in her brain, but Jax wasn't going to like it.

Not. One. Little. Bit.

Eighteen hours and one restless night's sleep later, Jax stared into the cooler full of live floral arrangements in the hospital gift shop and rubbed sweaty palms on his slacks. Did he dare give Daci flowers? Not red roses, of course. Majorly inappropriate. Daisies or carnations were nice. They were casual yet attractive, but they were still flowers—something a boyfriend would give, not a coworker, unless it were a group of coworkers.

Rey had hit him up to chip in on the live plant the Marshals Service sent up this morning, and he was glad to be included, but that generic gift wasn't enough. A part of him wanted—no, needed—to give her something that was just from him. But, no, flowers were not the thing.

Jax turned away from the cooler and scanned the other items available in the gift shop. There were magazines or books, but he didn't know what she liked to read. Did she enjoy games like sudoku or word find or crossword puzzles? He shook his head. Those were mundane gifts. Daci was special, and she deserved something special, something that said he appreciated her as an extraordinary human being without suggesting romance. But what might that something be?

His gaze fell on a collection of journaltype notebooks with zippered leather covers. Nearby, stood a rack displaying packets of pens in assorted bright-colored inks. He stepped closer, and his heart gave a little jump. A scripture verse was embossed on the turquoise cover of one notebook. It was Philippians 4:13: "I can do everything through Him who gives me strength." In church this morning, the pastor had referred to this verse in his sermon, pointing out that our weakest moments provided the greatest opportunity for God to show Himself strong.

Perfect! Daci was the strongest woman he'd ever met—and that was saying something—but everyone needed to lean on the Lord, especially when life had knocked them down. The notebook would remind her that help through Christ was as close as her next breath. And it would hopefully tell her that the person who gave her the notebook was also available to help.

Jax paid for his purchase of notebook and pens, had them wrap the gift and attached a small get-well-soon card, and then he headed for the elevator. All the way up to Daci's floor, his heart pounded like he'd just run around the block. Would he read delight on her face when she opened his present or would he receive a polite thank-you for an offering that struck no chord? And why did it matter so much to him to please her?

The closer he got to her door, the slower his feet moved and the less sure of his gift selection he became. He shoved the second-guessing away as he purposefully scanned the environment for any threat to Daci, but the comings and goings of staff and patients appeared routine and ordinary. At least the local PD had two officers stationed at Daci's door, not just one.

Jax quickened his pace. Daci might not know yet about Serena and Chase going missing or about other overnight developments. He had a lot to tell her. If he was in her place, he would want a full report, not mollycoddling.

He stopped outside her door and showed his badge to the officers. Their gazes remained hard and questioning. Rather than being annoyed, he was grateful that they were being suspicious after yesterday's deputy impersonation. Thankfully, the actual deputy who'd brought Jax's Malibu to the hospital—and whose uniform had been stolen by the attacker—had not been killed, only clobbered cold, bound and gagged and stuffed into the trunk of the assailant's car. He'd recover from his injury faster than he'd live down the humiliation.

"Jaxton Williams. Daci Marlowe is my partner," he told the officers.

One of them jerked a nod. "We've been told to let you through."

The other chuckled. "You might as well join the party."

"Party?"

"Marlowe has a family reunion going on, and that bunch read us the riot act about keeping her safe."

A burst of male and female laughter carried to Jax through the door, and his heart fell. Daci's siblings must be in there. Sure, he was glad they'd responded promptly to the news of her injury, and he had to count their caring a good thing, but he wouldn't be able to present his gift to Daci privately. His palms went damp again.

Man up, Williams.

He hauled in a deep breath, gave a brief rap on the door and then pressed through into the room. Five pairs of brown eyes all but nailed him to the wall, and he halted just over the threshold. Daci broke into a grin. The head of her bed had been raised so she was in a semisitting position. Her bright hair was pulled back loosely and formed a lush halo around her face, where she had regained a bit of healthy color.

"Sibs—" Daci waved toward him "—this is Jaxton Williams, my temp partner in the Marshals Service."

A sturdily built young man of medium height with a thick head of light brown hair stepped forward and thrust out a square hand. "I'm Nate, nerdy dentist and rabble-rouser extraordinaire. Thanks for looking after our mamasis." His eyes twinkled behind the lenses of his glasses.

Jax took the hand and received a firm shake. "My pleasure. She's an excellent deputy and very courageous."

"Tell us about it," said one of the young women with a pixie build and a waterfall of flaxen hair. She was seated at Daci's bedside, leaning one elbow on the mattress. "I'm Amalie. Ditto on the thanks."

"And I'm Noah," said a jeans-clad fellow seated in the corner with an ankle propped on the opposite knee. The guy was Nate's mirror image minus the glasses but adding a five-o'clock shadow around his jaw. "News journalist and rabble-rouser double-extraordinaire."

"Says you!" his twin hooted.

"Get a life, you two," said another woman, rushing toward Jax. "How-de-do and shake my hand is not going to work for the guy who saved our mamasis's life." The young woman threw her arms around him and kissed his cheek with a noisy smack. She stepped back and gazed up at him with a sober assessment that belied her light demeanor. "I'm Ava, and in case you haven't guessed, I'm the true enthusiast in this bunch."

"Pleased to meet Daci's family." Jax said each person's name around the room with an accompanying nod.

"Well done!" Ava clapped. "But you might have a bit of a challenge if you meet Nate and Noah dressed identically—Nate with his contacts in and Noah clean shaven. Even Amalie and I occasionally get it wrong, but never Dace. She knows them cold every time."

Jax laughed. "I can believe that. Not much gets past her."

"And what might you have behind your back?" Amalie wagged a slender finger at him. "Do I suspect correctly that you have a present for our mamasis?"

Jax gave a start. He hadn't realized he'd tried to hide the gift. Slowly, he brought the package to the front.

Ava let out a tiny squeal, and if such noises could be tasteful and understated, this one was. "Let's see what you've gotten her. I love presents—even if they're not for me."

"Yes, let's see," Nate echoed with considerably less enthusiasm.

He and Noah were gazing at him like skeptical employers at a new applicant. Jax bottled a smile. He totally got the protective instinct.

Too bad he couldn't reassure them he wasn't interested in their sister in *that* way. Any protesting would leave the opposite impression. Besides, he might be lying.

"Down, boys!" Daci said with a chuckle.

The slight gasp at the end of the sound told Jax that she was still in a good deal of pain. To be expected, and yet the knowledge sent a pang through him.

"*Is* that for me?" She nodded at the package.

"Just a little something." He stepped up to her bed and handed her the gift.

"Thank you."

Jax smiled as she ripped through the paper with no fussy peeling of the tape. So like her get-to-the-punch-line personality. She pulled out the notebook and packet of pens and stared, wide-eyed.

"Do you like it?"

Jax mentally kicked himself. Why had he let those words pop out of his mouth like some insecure teenager?

She raised her eyes to his. "I do." She shook herself with a little gasp—pain or self-awareness, he couldn't tell. "I mean, this is great. The perfect thing. You have no idea."

Something like a collective exhale sighed from Daci's siblings, reminding Jax of their presence. He cleared his throat and backed away from the bed.

"You really *don't* know," Ava said quietly.

"Our mamasis is a doodler," Amalie added.

"A what?" Jax looked from one to the other.

Face flaming, Daci hugged the journal to her chest. "It's a stress reliever. I doodle on paper, in frost on windows, on chalkboards, wherever I can make designs, while I give my emotions an outlet and let my brain loose. You know, to get free-form ideas. And then I write those ideas down. Weird, huh?"

"No, cool," he told her. "Way cool. Glad I got it right."

"Me, too."

They exchanged grins.

Daci sobered. "What's the update?"

Jax opened his mouth, but withheld the words as he glanced around at the audience present.

"Okay, sibs!" Amalie smacked her palms together. "We need to let these two alone to talk shop."

"Shop. *Right*." Ava giggled.

The journalist rose and yawned while stretching his arms wide. "I need a serious date with a pillow."

"Noah flew the red-eye last night from London," Daci said. "He called me from Heathrow airport before he took off, and I told him he didn't need to leave England, but here he is."

Her brother leaned over and pecked her on the cheek. "Couldn't beat any of us away with a stick, you know."

"I'm grateful. Hope I didn't ruin your chances at the story you went overseas to get."

"Had that wrapped up a couple days ago. I was just sightseeing. No problem."

With similar words of support, the other three gently hugged their sister then headed for the door.

"Hey, Jaxton," Nate said, holding the door as the others stepped out.

"Jax to my friends."

"Jax it is." The younger man flashed a quick smile. "Keep us in the loop. If there's anything we can do to help…" His voice trailed off, not with uncertainty, but rather with a wordless warning not to keep secrets regarding their sister's safety.

Noah popped his head back into the room. "Double ditto."

Jax gave them a brief salute and a nod. The door closed behind them, and he turned toward Daci, who was shaking her head.

"Not too subtle, are they?" She huffed through her nose. "I see I'm in for some hovering."

"Suffer on." Jax chuckled. "They're a great bunch. You did an awesome job on them."

"I—" She hesitated. "I did what I could. Grandma helped when she was allowed near us. But being around you with your steady faith, and now coming so close to death myself, it's made me rethink some things. I'm starting to realize that her faithful prayers probably did the most good of all."

She bowed her head and plucked at the sheet drawn up to her waist. "I'm really proud of my siblings, you know. They've taken to heart what Grandma and I told them about becoming productive citizens in this world—not just lolling around a swimming pool, sipping drinks handed to them by servants paid for with money they never lifted a finger to earn."

Jax cocked his head. "It's not a bad thing to employ people."

"No, but it's a bad thing to believe you're entitled to have others wait on you like you were born superior to other human beings. I'm sad to say, a couple of Marlowe generations forgot how to be real."

Jax pulled a chair up to her bedside and sat down. "Clearly, there were others in your ancestry who knew how to handle money."

"True enough." She smiled. "The Marlowes did well for themselves in the early years of this country, but we would have been bankrupt decades ago if not for the foresight of my great-grandfather. He was quite a businessman and doubled the family's considerable fortunes in his lifetime, but his only child was—according to the wording in great-grandfather's will—a 'dissolute rascal.' So, he stipulated that the properties and principal of the estate be under the control of a board of trustees until such time as they decide with unanimous vote to pass control to a Marlowe they deem capable of 'wisely handling material wealth.' Again, that was my great-grandfather's wording."

"I wouldn't be surprised if they decide that about you," Jax said.

Daci shook her head. "I don't want the headache of managing all those assets and property. It would be a full-time job. I'm quite comfortable the way things are. Annually, the interest on the principal is doled out to the direct descendants through trust funds each of us comes into at adulthood. The sum is quite generous, but when I was growing up, it seemed as if by the end of each year we were living like paupers until the next replenishment, which gives you an idea how my parents handled their money.

"My siblings have all come into their trust funds now, but they live like regular folks. In fact, they prefer a modest lifestyle—well, modest compared to what we could do. We haven't discussed it—we don't need to—but I know their extra cash is being used in ways that help others, not just themselves. *That's* what wealth is for." She sucked in a breath.

"Are you hurting?" Jax put a hand on her arm.

"No more than I should be." She frowned. "Why do I do this?"

"Do what?"

"Yammer on to you about my family stuff. You're too easy to talk to, Jax. Forgive me, and let's talk about the job."

"No forgiveness necessary." Jax pulled up a chair and sat at her bedside. "Your family is fascinating...and admirable, too."

"Admirable?" Daci snorted. "The past couple of generations of Marlowes tacked the prefix 'dys' onto 'functional' on an epic scale."

"All the more reason to admire the way you and your siblings have turned out."

"Thank you. I appreciate those kind words."

The depth of sincere gratitude in her gaze pierced Jax's heart. What he wouldn't give to take this woman in his arms and kiss away her doubts and fears! He could be glad her wounded condition prevented any impulsive behavior on his part.

Daci's intense expression relaxed into one of cool professionalism. "My guard detail outside the door told me the deputy who had his uniform stolen is concussed but recovering. Now I want to know how Serena and Chase are doing after that rude shock yesterday."

Jax dropped his gaze, lips pressed together. "What?"

He met her sharp look. "They've gone missing. No one has seen them since the park."

Her eyes popped wide. "Naylor got to them?"

"Unknown. She could have freaked out and decided to do a runner."

Daci pursed her lips. "Possible, but I'd go to the witness stand saying she'd only do that if she felt it was the best thing to protect Chase."

"Glad we're on the same page with that idea. Could be important when she's tracked down and consequences are discussed."

"Any sign of where she could be?"

"Her car was found early this morning parked in front of a convenience store. One of our guys interviewed the attendant who was on duty last night. The attendant told him a jittery young woman fitting Serena's description came in, bought a few snacks and a soda, then went back outside. She paced on the sidewalk, nibbling at a candy bar, until another car pulled up. At that point, she took something out of the back of her vehicle, but he didn't see what—or who, assuming it was Chase in his car seat—and got into the other car. Then they drove off."

"Someone picked her and Chase up?"

"For all we know, it could have been someone taking her to Naylor. We're doing everything we can to find the vehicle, but we don't have much of a description to go on."

"Grrr!" Her hands fisted. "I wish I could be out there helping to find them."

Jax covered one of her fists with his hand. "I wish you could be, too, but we have to get to the bottom of your case first."

Daci let out a sigh. "Anyone pry more information out of the guy who tried to smother me yesterday?"

"A little. He says the bounty on you is being handled through a professional broker who calls himself The Connection. He's got quite a reputation among those looking for murder-by-hire jobs."

"Who is this guy?"

"That's just it. Nobody ever meets with the person face-to-face. He uses a system of codes printed in newspapers, secret drop spots and encrypted electronic communication worthy of the CIA."

"Whoever wants me dead is no two-bit

hood if they're using such a sophisticated and costly approach."

"Exactly. Who in your life have you royally angered that has those kinds of resources? And how might that person be connected to your uncle and the small-time crook turned restauranteur who killed your grandmother? There's got to be a connection."

Daci threw up her hands. "I haven't a clue. Over the years, I've had a few slick suitors who thought it would be a good idea to enhance their wallets with my money through marriage. But they weren't that heartbroken by my rejection that they'd want to kill me. And the last one walked away years ago. They've long since moved on to easier game."

"I still think this business must be linked with whoever masterminded the carjacking ring that went after your Lexus."

She frowned. "Could my uncle have been part of the ring?"

Jax didn't answer the question. It sounded rhetorical, anyway.

"Makes sense." She bit her lower lip and looked away. "No wonder he was so vicious about trying to cast the blame on me for Grandma's death. Anything but face his own guilt."

"Are you sure you don't have a degree in psychology?" Jax said softly.

"I do, actually." She turned her gaze on him, amusement lighting her face. "I earned it completely online while I was shepherding my brat-pack through the maze of adolescence."

Jax chuckled. "You never cease to amaze me."

"I think I'm going to do it again." Her gaze intensified. "I have a plan to catch the person who wants me dead, but I'm going to need bait."

"What bait?"

"Me."

EIGHT

Jax's face went red then chalk white. "Don't joke," he bit out.

It was the reaction Daci had expected, but still it was exasperating not to have her ideas taken seriously.

She grabbed his sleeve. "What other bait can there be if the goal is my death?"

"What are you going to do? Stake yourself out like a sacrificial goat? You'll only draw the hirelings, not the person behind the contract."

"First of all, when I'm released I'm going home to recuperate."

"Finally, you're talking sense. Between the Marshals Service and the PD, we'll have your apartment covered."

"No. I'm going *home*—to the family estate in Boston, where I grew up. The place is a walled fortress with an excellent electronic security system. I know. The trustees have pretty much given me free rein around there, and I had it installed myself. Add some manpower from law enforcement, and it will be way easier to defend than my duplex. Besides, I don't want to draw any danger down on my neighbors here."

"Good thinking." Jax nodded. "I'm not a bit surprised that your considerations go beyond your own well-being. That's the kind of person you are."

Daci ignored the little pulse ka-bump his praise elicited. "You're still not getting it." She started to lean forward, then pulled back at the stab of pain in her abdomen. If only she wasn't so weak and hurting she'd feel a lot more confident in her plan, but it didn't pay to let Jax in on her doubts.

"I believe the person who wants me dead lives in Boston. Even though the crime boss behind the carjacking ring was never uncovered, several chop shops were shut down in the course of the police investigation, and investigators concluded that Boston was the nexus of the operation. Samuel Clayhorn was originally from Boston, and my uncle lived there all of his life. All roads lead to Beantown."

He leaned closer, brow crinkled. "I follow you so far."

"I need to invite my killer into my fortress and let him try for me in person."

Jax jerked back against his chair so fiercely the legs bucked and clattered against the floor. "Of all the harebrained… How… We don't even know who…"

His spluttering would have been kind of cute if the lack of confidence in her planning skills wasn't so annoying.

"Stop thinking like a protector and start thinking like a hunter." She crossed her arms, then thought better of the effort and let them drop to her sides. A nap sounded like a winner right now, but she had to get Jax on board with her idea first. Otherwise, while she took her nap, he'd start moving mountains to keep her plan from going into effect. "Haven't we all come to the conclusion that these attempts on my life must be linked to my past?"

Jax offered a reluctant nod.

"Okay, then, let's follow that reasoning. Whoever is after me can afford a big bounty, but doesn't have access to his or her own stable of hired killers, like your usual crime boss. Sounds like some of the high flyers my parents hung out with, right? More than a few of them didn't come by their money honestly. How unlikely is it that the kingpin behind the carjacking ring was among them, and now that Clayhorn has drawn attention back to that old crime, he or she thinks I know something that could point the finger at them?"

He pursed his lips. "Possible. Maybe even probable."

"Okay, then, I'm going to throw a party and invite them all to attend. Boston high society is pretty insular, and I know who they are, even though I've never socialized with them—other than making a few friends in the private schools I attended. The so-called Boston Brahmins will be falling all over themselves to accept an invitation back onto a property they've been barred from for years. I'll give myself a couple of weeks to get some strength back, and—"

"A couple of weeks? You heard the doctor. A month, minimum."

"We can't wait that long. Make that, *I* can't wait that long. It's not fair to the Marshals Service or the PD to expect them to extend protection for such a long period. I could hire my own bodyguards, but living like that would drive me nutty. Besides, any of them might find the bounty on me appealing. The longer we wait, the more time we give one of those hirelings to find a way to get to me. No, we need to create an opportunity quite soon, tailor-made for the one who's paying them—an opening too perfect to resist, even if it means getting his own hands dirty for once. How about a party that might be the social event of the season? Invitation only. Exclusive access. We control who goes in and out, and—"

"Hold it!" Jax held up a hand, palm out. "That scenario reeks. You've never been a party girl or close with the people who were your parents' friends. Why would they believe you're suddenly hosting them at a social event, especially when you're recuperating from an attempt on your life? Coming from you, this can't be some random soiree. Only a *cause* will be believable."

Daci grinned. "You're on the right track."

He shook a finger at her. "Don't think I don't know what you're doing, Ms. Clever. You're recruiting me through brainstorming."

"Is it working?"

"Maybe." He grunted. "What sort of cause have you come up with?"

"A charity auction. Boston society has been salivating for years to get their hands on some of the old treasures stored in the Marlowe family mansion. Off-loading some of them has been in my mind for a while, and I don't anticipate any trouble convincing the board of directors to sanction the auction in order to establish a charitable foundation."

"What organization will benefit from the

proceeds? That's got to be believable, too, as something you would really care about."

"Remember my neighbors in the group home talking about this spiritual and social program at their church for mentally, socially and emotionally challenged adults? Everything from FAS to Down syndrome to autism?"

"I do. What was that called?" He snapped his fingers. "Uniquely Made! That was it."

"I'm totally, legitimately jazzed over the idea." Her heart beat faster. "In fact, I'd like to see the program assist these special-needs people from birth to the grave by creating a foundation offering grants to churches and nonprofits willing to run such programs. Naomi Minch's day care would be eligible to apply because they are a faith-based nonprofit that offers care and developmental assistance to the youngest of the mentally and emotionally challenged."

Jax's face lit. "My organization could apply, too. We've been looking for ways to move beyond legal aid for this vulnerable segment of the population. My church would probably hop on the opportunity, too."

Daci giggled, holding her side against a sharp pang. "Methinks the man has discovered his enthusiasm."

"About the foundation." He scowled. "Not about you setting yourself up as a target."

"I don't have to set myself up. I'm already a target. I'm just being proactive about where and when the attempt is made."

His lips thinned. "If I could argue any further with that logic, I would."

"So, you're in? I'm going to need you to commit your next couple of weekends to come and help move and catalog the items I want to auction. I won't hire outside help. Too risky."

"Too right! What about your siblings? Won't they want to be part of sorting through things?"

"Of course. They'll be there as much as they can. But Nate's got an impending wedding and a new dentistry practice to think about, Noah could get assigned who-knows-where at any time, and my sisters are nearing finals week at Dartmouth. Their time to pitch in is as limited as yours."

"Don't make assumptions involving my time." His gaze went stern.

Daci's heart fell. If she failed to recruit Jax, how would she pull this off?

The corners of his lips curled in a smile that could only be called sly. "I have a lot of vacation coming, and I might consider using it for a good cause if…"

"If what?" She narrowed her eyes at him.

"A little quid pro quo. You remain in the hospital to the limits of the doctor's recommendation, *and* you wait at least three weeks after your release before attempting to host an auction. In return, I will not only devote my full attention to auction preparations, but I will pick you up from the hospital on the day of your release and personally drive you to Boston. Any PD officers or deputies that want to tag along are welcome to do so, but I won't rest easy until I see with my own eyes that I've gotten you to a place that is as safe as we can make it."

Daci opened her mouth, and Jax laid a finger against her lips. The gentle touch sent a delightful tingle down her spine.

"No argument."

"I wasn't going to argue." She folded her hands primly in her lap. "I was going to say thank you. There's a guest wing at the big house that you can commandeer for your own, or a pool house if you prefer."

"Sounds good." He rose to his feet. "Which button do I push to settle this bed down into sleeping position? You look like you're about to pass out."

"Thank you again, kind sir. Your insult is received in the spirit in which it was given."

"Not an insult. A reality check."

He was right. Daci managed a weary smile as Jax found the button and lowered the bed. Oh, did it feel good to settle back against her pillow. Her eyelids were weighted with bricks.

"I'll be back to check on you this evening."

The comforting words followed her toward slumber. At last she could let her mind rest. She and Jax were going to pull this off. No, not just she and Jax. Not even with the help of the law-enforcement team that would need to be involved.

God, I haven't been following You like I should, but if You're listening, then please, for the sake of my grandma, help us make this happen. Help justice to be served. And help Serena and Chase, wherever they are.

Her mental amen trailed away into the oblivion of sleep.

Five days later, clad in gentle-waisted leggings and an oversize top, Daci allowed hospital staff to help her into a wheelchair while Jax boxed up the flowers, plants and gifts she'd collected during her stay. A pair of deputies waited outside the door to escort them down to Jax's vehicle. Settling into the chair, she released the breath she'd been holding against the pain of movement. The wound in her side had healed significantly, but the doctor had been right about the bruising in her abdomen.

Even taking a deep breath could shoot pangs through her.

Maybe she wasn't up to this auction thing. She glanced at Jax, standing ready at the door. No way could she voice her doubts. He'd already gotten the time off, and had gone to a lot of trouble to ensure his cases were being handled properly in his absence. Ready or not, she had to be all in.

"Ready?" he asked with a smile, as if he'd heard her thoughts.

"As I'll ever be." She grinned back. Might as well put a good face on it.

Soon she was installed in the cushy passenger seat of a new-smelling Audi RS7, her purse snuggled next to her for easy access. As they left the hospital parking lot, a marked PD car in the lead and an unmarked Marshals Service heavy-duty pickup in the rear, she ran her hand over the leather seat.

"You traded in your Malibu."

His gaze scanning the road and surrounding environment, Jax nodded. "This operation called for something with superb handling and a whole lot more get-up-and-go."

"I see," she said. "While lolling around in bed, I finally had the opportunity to look you up on my laptop." She hesitated. This wasn't the time to bring up certain things she'd found out—the things that had hurt him so badly—so she chose another topic. "Why didn't you tell me your family comes from old money, also?"

He shrugged, never taking his eyes from the road. "Didn't seem relevant. Neither of us cares about the power and status money can bring, though it sure did come in handy when I bought this vehicle." He chuckled and patted his steering wheel. "I imagine a generation or two ago, my bunch would have been considered parvenus by your bunch. Sam Walton types with humble beginnings, who hauled themselves up by the bootstraps through blue-collar industry."

Daci grinning. "You're probably right about our forefathers, but I respect that you work because you want to benefit society, not just because you have to make a living."

"Ditto. I've seen grit and integrity in you since the day we met."

Daci's insides turned to gooey mush. A vision of his firm lips on hers flitted through her head, stirring her pulse. Honestly, this being-wounded business had turned her into a complete basket case.

Blinking away fantasies, she gazed around, taking in the passing environment. Offices, hotels, restaurants and businesses whizzed by on both sides. They were on I-291 heading north toward I-90. All vehicle behavior in their vicinity appeared normal and nonthreatening.

"No sign of Serena and Chase?" she asked. "Or Naylor?"

With her whacked-out emotions, it was safer to talk about business.

"Afraid not. No more Naylor sightings, and as for Serena and Chase, the trail stops cold at the convenience store." Their vehicle with escort merged onto I-90. "Why don't you put that seat back and grab a little shut-eye. Should be smooth sailing from here to Boston."

He must have noticed how her eyelids kept drooping. Unbelievable how weak she was. She had to regain her strength, and the best route to that goal seemed to be plenty of rest.

Moments after she closed her eyes, a sharp rat-a-tat-tat jerked her awake. Her eyes sprang open. It hadn't been moments. At least an hour and a half had passed. The Boston skyline filled her gaze. Checking the rearview mirror, she took in the Marshals Service vehicle behind them fishtailing and falling back. Her eyes widened and her heart stalled.

In the lane on the driver's side of the Audi, an armored Humvee roared toward them, an automatic weapon clearly visible in the passenger's arms.

* * *

Jax's grip throttled the steering wheel. They were under attack on a busy interstate, and their rear guard was already disabled. The RS7's 560-horsepower, twin-turbocharged V8 engine had better show its worth pronto. He rammed the gas pedal, whipping into the next lane away from the Humvee, and sped past the marked police car as if it were standing still. In his side-view mirror, he noted the police car's lights come on. No doubt the officers had notified HQ of the attack in progress. They could count on backup. But how soon? There was no time to wait around for reinforcements to arrive.

"Tighten your seat belt, Daci. Pardon my sarcasm, but this could get way more than fun."

With one hand guiding his vehicle's sprint away from danger, he stuck the other hand under his jacket and pulled out his pistol. He deposited the weapon in the cup holder, muzzle down for quick access, then returned to driving with both hands. Out of the corner of his eye, he caught his passenger's movements as Daci reach into her purse and come out with her service pistol. Drawing the heavy weapon to herself, she gasped and winced in obvious pain.

"Whoa! You're not strong enough to think about pulling the trigger."

"Needs must," she said, and laid the gun across her lap.

Jax scowled and concentrated on putting distance between them and the Humvee. Strange that the attacker's vehicle wasn't speeding up to follow them, but staying with the police car. A recurring pop-pop-pop indicated an exchange of gunfire.

Or maybe not so strange.

They were in the farthest right lane of the freeway, coming up on an entrance ramp. Merging toward them roared a second Humvee. No need to guess whether the occupants were armed to the teeth.

In a split second, he checked his rearview mirror. Because of the firefight behind them, his freeway lane was clear to at least fifty yards back. He rammed down on the brake pedal. Brakes squealed, rubber burned, but the RS7 responded like a champ. His body slammed against his seat belt. Daci screamed, and Jax's heart squeezed in on itself, knowing the pain the move must have caused her. But he couldn't bring himself to truly regret it.

Better a moment of pain than sudden death.

The Humvee's momentum barreled it onto the freeway ahead of them. Gunfire burst from occupants in the monster vehicle's back seat, but the bullets merely shot sparks from the tarmac in front of the Audi's nose. So far, so good. The tactic must have disoriented the Humvee's driver because the vehicle wavered back and forth on the road, even crossing partly into the next lane, where the driver of a little hatchback laid on his horn.

Better fade back, buddy, Jax mentally warned the driver as he pressed the accelerator on the RS7. Only a few yards to go, and they'd grab an exit ramp, taking them off the freeway. The Humvee currently engaging the police officers could potentially take the same exit, but they'd have to be quick about it. The attackers who'd been tricked into point position had already missed the turnoff and were out of the equation. The odds had suddenly improved.

Jax took the curve onto the exit. Another wave of bullets stitched the rear driver's side of the RS7. Jax fought the wheel as his peripheral vision caught sight of an attacker leaning out a window of the Humvee to make crazy-angled shots. A moment later, the curve of the exit took them out of range, and he hauled in a ragged breath.

"We need to take a less obvious route to your estate. How about—"

"Follow my directions, Jax. I know Boston like the back of my hand, including the most devious ways to get where we're going. Awesome driving, by the way."

He laughed, a giddy sensation flowing through him—whether from the compliment coming from her lips or the relief of being beyond gunshot range. For the moment.

"Turn left at the light," she said. "We'll zigzag through this city like we're dodging snipers…because we are…and come up on the old Marlowe homestead from the rear."

Her voice sounded thin. Jax glanced over at her. She was holding herself stiffly, and her face had lost color. He could ask her if she was in pain, but that would only belabor the obvious. That sudden brake job would have wrenched her bruised insides something fierce.

Jax returned his gaze to the two-lane road they were on. Small businesses were giving way to moderate-income residences.

"I think we'll be okay until we get close to our destination. Rey's fears about a mole in the Marshals Service are well-founded. Clearly, our hunters knew when the escort was to meet us at the hospital, and they're going to know exactly where we're taking you. As we preplanned, deputies and PD officers will be stationed around the perimeter of your estate, but I'm not trusting their locations won't be known to the bad guys who will also be waiting for us."

"Nobody is going to anticipate the way we'll come in," Daci said, "but we'll have to go it on foot a short way." She shifted in her seat and sucked in a soft breath, then let it out slowly, carefully. "You may have to help me some."

"You've got it."

"That mole in the service makes everything so much more complicated."

"Maddening that we don't know who it is. That person has a lot to be accountable for— Liggett Naylor's escape, betraying you repeatedly to whoever is trying to kill you, and who knows what other cases have been blown by this rat."

"Make up your mind, Williams. And, while you're at it, take a right turn here."

"Make up my mind?" Jax shot her a questioning look as he navigated the corner.

"Exactly what sort of rodent we're dealing with—a mole or a rat?"

"Very funny, Marlowe."

His heart lifted. Her humor was lame, but at least she was making jokes.

Daci continued to give him directions, and he continued to obey them, even as he kept a close eye on their surroundings. Every passing vehicle was a potential threat. They wove through some of the most historically rich neighborhoods in Boston, including Beacon Hill, but relaxing and enjoying the tour was not on the agenda—especially when they skirted through a few less-than-savory areas.

"I'm really bothered that Serena and Chase are still missing," Daci said. "I've been racking my brains for any clue about where they could be, and I just now remembered something she said at lunch before we went to the park."

Jax stiffened. "You know where they are?"

"No, but I have a big, fat clue about who might be the mole in the service."

She told him Naylor's remarks to Serena about having "the system" in his pocket and having "it" on a leash.

"System? It?" Jax echoed. "I-T!"

"Bingo!"

"Randy Lathrop?" Jax let out a whistle under his breath. "Our desk clerk? He's the only person in the Springfield office that could remotely come under that designation."

"Unless the mole is stationed at Boston HQ. I'm leaning in that direction. They have a designated IT person who could access absolutely anything in the system."

"You have a point. Call Rey's cell, and clue him in. He'll carry the ball from there."

"I'm on it."

Daci got on the phone, and Jax continued to watch their environment. They were entering an expensive neighborhood where the value of the gated homes ran in the millions. As she talked to their boss, she continued to point Jax this direction and that, weaving them deeper into the heart of affluence. They had to be drawing near the Marlowe estate.

He slowed the car and kept scanning the area for anything or anyone out of place. Who knew if the middle-aged woman wearing designer workout clothes and walking a coiffured purebred spaniel was an assassin? He held his breath until they passed her. His ears began to pick up the sound of a helicopter in the distance. Not a strange noise in a city where anything from Coast Guard to news, law enforcement or emergency choppers were in the air continually.

Daci pocketed her phone. "I think we've finally managed to make DC Reynolds happy about something,"

"Happy?"

"And mad enough to stomp an alligator at the same time. If I'm right and Reynolds can find the proof to back it up then I don't envy that mole when he catches the person."

That deep helicopter whump-whump grew

louder, closing in on their location. Jax glanced upward and spotted the bird. For sure, not the Coast Guard. Not law enforcement or emergency services, either. In fact, he could make out no logo on the chopper's body. Not a good sign. Private helicopters were a lot less common, and this one could well carry enemies.

"We've got company closing in above us."

"I hear it," Daci answered. "We're almost there. Hang a left and hit the gas. We're going to ditch the car."

"Hop out and make a run for it in the open? An ordinary skeet shooter could take us out, much less the kind of marksmen we're dealing with."

"Trust me."

No question about that. He did.

They took the turn, and he floored it. Ahead, the road ended in a wall of dense woods. Behind them, the chopper dipped lower and swooped close. A shot rang out, and the rear windshield shattered. Daci yelped.

"Are you hit?" Jax cried out.

"Don't worry about me—keep going straight into the trees!"

Swallowing his Adam's apple back into place, Jax did as he was told. They were about to ram a thicket of tall bushes head-on, but risking death by bush beat a sure demise by bullet.

The Audi's nose ripped into the foliage. The paint job and undercarriage screamed as branches and twigs ravaged them. They went airborne for a bare second and then landed with a solid thump that tested the suspension system to the max.

"Whoa!" Jax applied the brakes.

They were headed down a slope into a ravine on a path barely wide enough for the sporty sedan to avoid sturdy tree trunks on either side. Above them, thick foliage guaranteed the occupants of the helicopter could no longer see them, but the sudden dimness after bright sunshine had Jax running half-blind, as well.

He needed to get this vehicle stopped before he slammed them head-on into one of these massive, old oak trees, but the rotting leaves on the forest floor were damp and slippery, offering little traction. Even the high-tech brake system on the RS7 was having a hard time gripping and holding. At last they slid to a fishtailing halt inches from the bottom of the ravine, where the Audi's nose would have bit the dirt, possibly setting off the airbags. Not a good scenario, given Daci's tender middle.

Shaking, Jax put the car into Park and looked over at his passenger. A narrow ray of light speared through the leaf canopy and il-

luminated her bright head. She slumped im-
mobile against the passenger door. Jax's pulse
stalled. Her chest rose and fell in slow breathing, but a trail of blood dripped from her chin
onto her shirt. How badly was she hurt? How
long would she keep breathing?

Jax's guts tore. A wail rent his throat. He
couldn't do this again—lose someone he loved
to an evil man's attack.

Loved? Where had that come from?

No time for navel-gazing. The aerial assault
had driven them to ground. The foot soldiers
would be on the way.

Jax grabbed his pistol and stuck it into his
shoulder holster. He shoved his door open
and climbed out onto the loamy-smelling forest floor. Eyes adjusting, he scanned his environment. Nothing but trees in sight, but by the
sound of it, the chopper still hovered overhead.
No doubt marking the spot for their buddies.
The activity would draw the attention of law
enforcement, too, but Daci and he couldn't wait
to see who arrived first.

Jax hurried around the vehicle and pulled
Daci's door open. Her torso tumbled sideways
into his arms. He caught her and wrapped his
arms around her. A peach scent from her hair
teased his nostrils.

"Hang in there, sweetheart."

He reached across her lap, undid her seat belt and lifted her from the car, allowing her service pistol to thump to the ground. She was in no condition to use it anyway. Kneeling, he kept an arm around her head and trunk, but laid her lower body on the ground. His gaze sought for the source of the blood.

There! A gash in the side of her head just below the temple. Not a bullet wound. Either a piece of flying glass had grazed her, or her head had slammed against the passenger-side window during their hectic descent into the ravine. Not a life-threatening injury, and the bleeding had already stopped on its own. The jouncing of her tender insides had probably done more damage than this small cut.

She stirred in his arms and groaned. Then her eyes popped open. Those deep brown depths engulfed him.

A trembling smile curved her lips. She lifted a hand and cupped his cheek. The touch sent rockets caroming around his insides.

"Did someone call me sweetheart?"

NINE

Gazing into Jax's concerned face hovering so near her own, Daci's heart danced to a song her sensible mind was powerless to turn off or tune out. So what if falling for this man was a bad idea. Her tender middle and pounding head squawked about the recent abuse they had suffered, but surely one kiss from him would be like healing balm.

His gaze darkened, and his face hovered over hers, drawing closer...closer. A thrill shivered through her. She shut her eyes, anticipating the touch of his lips on hers.

In the distance, a twig snapped and they both jerked. Daci's eyes sprang wide open. Jax's head went up, nostrils flared, gaze seeking, like a stag that had been alerted to danger. Had an innocent animal made that noise or a hunter after human prey?

"We need to go," he whispered.

"I know."

Did as much regret tinge her voice as lurked behind the gaze he turned upon her?

His focus shifted, and he snatched something from the ground. Her service pistol.

"I'm carrying this." He tucked it into the waistband of his pants. "Are you able to walk?"

"Watch me." Daci gritted her teeth against the pain as Jax helped her to her feet. "We don't have far to go. This way." She pointed up the ravine.

"Lean on me, then."

Walking quickly, sometimes stumbling against roots and stones hidden by the leaf mulch, sometimes stepping over fallen logs, they put distance between themselves and the disabled vehicle—the first spot pursuers would look for them. Daci's ears sought telltale signs of that pursuit, but found only the swish of the breeze playing among the leaves and the pat-pat of their footfalls against the damp earth.

Pain and exhaustion clouded her brain, but she shook them away. She *had* to remain alert.

"There!" She leaned against Jax's supporting arm and pointed to the side of the ravine.

He stopped abruptly. She wobbled on her feet, and he steadied her.

"There where?" His eyebrows went up. "I don't see anything but a bunch of ivy creepers dangling off the end of a rock ledge."

"Good. I'm glad this spot hasn't changed. That's all our enemies will see if we slip carefully behind the veil of creepers, disturbing them as little as possible. Let me go first."

His arm tightened around her shoulders. "We're not going to take cover behind a few flimsy vines."

"No, we're not." She grinned up at him. "Trust me again."

He groaned. "Do I have a choice, mystery woman?"

A soft giggle left her throat, abruptly stilled by the sound of a dull thump and a snarled curse somewhere back along their trail. Another voice shushed the foul mouth. Definitely enemies, not law enforcement. Allies would be calling their names, not attempting stealth.

"Methinks our hunters are more at home in the urban jungle than the real woods," she whispered, and left the comfort of Jax's steadying arms.

Her aching middle begged her to crumple into a ball and hug it tight, but she ignored the inner whining as she stepped to the curtain of vines and parted them. A dank odor all but overwhelmed her, wafting from the black hole of a drainage pipe that gaped in the side of the ravine. Behind her, Jax's sharp intake of breath said he'd seen the pipe, too.

Before he could say a word, she crawled into the opening, giving him no option but to follow. The creepers fell together, encasing them in utter blackness. She crawled onward, who-knows-what squishing beneath her hands and knees.

"What about wild critters?" Jax hissed as he stayed on her heels.

"If there are any, they'll have to get out of our way," she murmured in reply.

She suppressed a shiver, partly from the dank chill, but also from the thought of meeting some rodent or reptile. Happily, the enclosed space didn't smell like skunk, so that possibility was remote.

The sharp snap of a breaking stick carried up the pipe, and Daci went still. Jax must have done the same, because the darkness went stone silent. Then a rustle betrayed him shifting positions. A soft click raised the hairs on Daci's arms. Beyond doubt he pointed a pistol, round chambered, toward the pipe's outlet. If any of their pursuers parted the veil of vines, he would shoot first and ask questions later—provided they remained alive to ask any.

Not-so-stealthy footfalls passed the pipe opening and faded away.

"Let's go," Jax whispered.

Without a word, she complied. The pipe

began to incline upward, and soon faint light appeared ahead. They arrived at a flat spot where the metal tube turned upward at a right angle. Above them, the perforated lid of a manhole cover allowed a few rays of sunshine to dispel the darkness. The rungs of a metal ladder led up to it.

Puffing and hugging her stomach, she sat huddled against the wall and turned her face toward the welcome light. Jax entered the upright pipe and stood to his feet.

"Let me rest a minute," she told him.

He knelt before her. "Where will we be when we climb out of here?"

"Believe it or not, we're under a road that has a right-of-way through Marlowe property. The woodland acreage on this side is ours, as are the estate house and grounds on the other side." She grimaced against a pang from her abused middle. "Good thing it isn't raining today. When it rains, the water flows through the pipe so hard that the vines on the other side never get to bond firmly with the rocks and soil beneath the pipe opening, leaving a curtain of growth that is easily parted to access the tube. My siblings and I found this out when we were playing in the woods."

Memories unfurled in Daci's mind. Happy ones. She smiled.

"We'd pack lunches and spend all day out here. Our parents never missed us, and the servants didn't care. We were out from under their feet. Eventually, nightfall would drive us, covered in dirt and the usual childhood scrapes and bruises, back to the toxic luxury of our home."

Daci basked in the tenderness flowing from Jax's gaze. He reached out and plucked something from her hair.

She stiffened. "What was that?"

"You don't want to know."

"A spider?" No doubt the little squeak at the end of the question betrayed her feelings about those creepy critters.

He just grinned. "Like I said, you don't want to know." He glanced upward. "Are you able to climb the ladder? I'll carry you if you like."

She shook her head. "No, you won't. I'll have to be up to the climb and a good sprint, too. You'll want a firearm drawn, because we're going to have to scurry across a small meadow and a half-moon driveway to the lych-gate."

"Lych-gate! We're in America, not the British countryside. On this side of the Atlantic, even the graveyards hardly ever have those stone-covered gateways."

"The Marlowes do, complete with a private graveyard *and* a chapel on one corner of the estate grounds. We weren't always an ungodly family. Our first immigrant ancestors came over not long after the *Mayflower*, with strong faith convictions that drove a wedge between them and their aristocratic relatives."

"Just when I think your family can't get any more surprising, you tell me something that proves me wrong." Shaking his head, Jax pulled out his phone. "I'm going to call Rey— have him tell the team stationed at the estate to lay down cover fire and open the gate for us."

Daci put a hand over his phone screen.

"What?" He blinked at her.

"If we're mistaken about the source of the leak, or if it hasn't been plugged yet, issuing orders through channels could be letting the bad guys in on our location."

Jax groaned. "It absolutely stinks not to be able to trust anyone."

"Except each other."

The words blurted out Daci's mouth with a burst of emotion so intense it shook her physically. The number of people she had ever totally trusted she could literally count on one hand—her siblings and her grandmother. Now, since Jax had entered her life, she would have to use a finger on her other hand for the tally. His gaze bored into her as if he'd heard the wonder and terror in her realization that the protective walls around her life had been breached by an outsider.

She yanked her focus from him, reached into a pocket of her shirt and pulled out a key. "Given the determination and resources of whoever is after me, I suspected we might need to stage a surprise entrance. This will unlock the gateway that is set into the high wall around the estate, and then we will be in the graveyard outside the chapel, which is part of the larger estate property. Once inside, we'll be safe from ground fire. If the chopper tries to swoop in, we can take cover in the chapel until our guys deal with it."

"Sounds like a plan. I'm going first," Jax said.

"You'll have to." She tucked the key into her pocket. "At the moment, I don't have the strength to move that manhole cover."

Steeling herself against the distraction of pain and a soul-deep weariness that urged her to collapse, Daci clung to a rung of the metal ladder while Jax shoved at the metal cover over their hidey-hole. *Was* she up to the sprint that would take them to some measure of safety? She couldn't guarantee it, but she had to try.

With a soft pop, the cover came loose, and Jax scraped it to the side. A waft of fresh air blew a little of the fog from Daci's brain. A distant *whump-whump-whump* let her know the helicopter was still up there, searching for them. Her pulse throbbed faster.

Gritting her teeth, she started up the ladder while Jax pulled himself to the surface in a low crouch. No gunfire greeted his appearance, and Daci's breathing eased marginally. Jax turned and helped her from the hole until she stood steady on the tarmac.

Sort of. She was nearing the end of her endurance. Willpower alone held her upright, and that could fail at any moment. If Jax was forced to carry her, he would be left defenseless. She couldn't let that happen.

"This way." She motioned toward a tall hedge of lilac bushes that lined the side of the road opposite the woods.

In the years since she'd last been this way, the bushes had become overgrown, a matter she'd see to remedying if she survived. Hopefully, the spot where she and her siblings used to sneak through remained less entwined than the rest of the hedge. She and Jax couldn't afford the delay of trotting up the open road to one of the entrances to the half-moon drive that swung by the lych-gate.

Daci hurried toward the runt of the bushes that marked the weakness in the living barrier. *Yes!* They were going to get scratched, but they could force their way through. Ducking her head, she plowed forward. The fulsome scent of blooming lilacs dizzied her mind. In a moment, she burst free, rubbing fresh scratches on her bare arms and entered a small meadow carpeted with blue and yellow wildflowers. A mere twenty yards or so distant, a stone gateway flanked by vine-covered walls beckoned.

She started forward only to be snatched backward by a strong arm and swept into the embrace of the lilac bushes. Pain streaked through her middle, but her outcry was absorbed in the sturdy shoulder that cradled her face.

"We've got company," Jax whispered in her ear. Overhead, the helicopter thundered near. "Unless they outright land, they shouldn't be able to see us."

Wordlessly, Daci nodded against him. He smelled like an oddly appealing mixture of damp soil, rotting leaves and his sophisticated, woodsy soap—a truly insignificant detail to notice in this critical moment, but inhaling his scent was like inhaling comfort and security. And if this turned out to be their last seconds on earth, what better way to spend them than here in his arms? She relaxed against him as a great lethargy seeped through every cell of her body.

"Go!" Jax abruptly pulled her out from the shelter of the bushes and began running toward the gate, half-carrying her with one arm, wielding his pistol with the other.

Daci fought to keep her feet under her. She had to contribute to this sprint, not be an anchor, but the effort was a losing battle. Her world faded to a gray blur. Shouts and gunshots rang out. Then nothing.

The moment Daci went limp, Jax dropped his pistol and swept her into his arms. Hugging her close, protecting her with his body, he lengthened his stride straight for the door in the wall. No time for evasive maneuvers. They'd either reach safety or they wouldn't.

From somewhere on his left flank, a man's voice hollered, followed by a gunshot. Then a second shot sounded—different caliber firearm—and someone yelped. Defenders against assassins? Who fired which shot and who was hurt? Couldn't concentrate on that now.

Just—get—to—that—door!

Overhead, chopper noises closed in again. Then a second aerial buzz saw joined the mix. Then a third. The din filled the atmosphere, yet seemed distant. Inconsequential. Jax was in his own cocoon with the rasp of his breathing, the rush of his pulse in his ears and the warmth of Daci's body hugged to his chest.

Only a few more yards!

A bullet blew a chip off the stone wall to his right, and a sharp pain grazed his ear, but they had made it to the wide wooden door. With his precious burden, he huddled into the gateway's overhang. Holding Daci against him with one arm, he sought for the key in her pocket with the opposite hand.

There!

He thrust it toward the keyhole, but the door suddenly sprang open. A pair of PD uniforms rushed past them, guns drawn, even as a set of arms attached to a familiar face yanked them through the portal.

Jax stood under a stone archway, breathing hard and clinging to Daci's limp form. His gaze scanned the thoroughly British church-yard and chapel that lay before him. Grave-stones, some of them quite ancient looking, dotted the lawn between him and the small building. A few more seconds outside the es-tate walls, and he and Daci would likely have been slated for headstones themselves.

His gaze fell on the man who'd pulled them to safety. "Noah, what are you doing here?"

"I live here when I'm not globetrotting. When we heard you two dropped out of sight on the run, I knew this entrance was where Mamasis would head." Face grim, he reached for Daci. "How badly is she hurt?"

Jax cuddled her closer, and the other man dropped his arms with a lift of his brows.

"She hasn't been shot again," Jax told him. "The blood is from a scrape when we crash-landed in the woods, but it's nothing serious. The real problem is that the chase was too much. She passed out. We need to get her some place where she can rest and be examined by a doctor."

"You, too." Noah pointed to the side of Jax's neck.

He hadn't noticed before, but warmth trickled down the side of his neck into his shirt line. "It's nothing. Just a nick."

Daci's journalist brother waved him to follow and set off through the churchyard. Stepping into the open, Jax's gaze swept the sky above them, but chopper sounds had grown distant. Only pristine blue, airbrushed with wispy clouds, filled his eyes.

A group of law-enforcement personnel rushed toward them—judging by the uniforms, a mix of PD and Marshals Service personnel.

"We're clear," the lead man said. "Our choppers are in pursuit of the suspects' bird, and two assailants outside have been apprehended."

Surrounded by defenders, Jax carried Daci across a broad, manicured lawn dotted with bushes and flower beds. Ahead, a brown brick Federal-style mansion ruled the landscape sprawled at its feet. Noah led them onto a cement patio and then through a pair of French doors into a large room furnished like a combination office and sitting room. The space left the impression of understated elegance, but there was no time to admire any decor as Daci's brother led them onward into a wide hallway and then to an immense foyer and a sweeping staircase.

Jax followed the leader briskly up the stairs, down another hallway and into a bedroom that screamed Daci with its color scheme of blues and browns. Tenderly, he settled her onto her bed and brushed strands of hair from her face. Her face was pale and drawn, but her chest rose and fell evenly.

"Hang in there, Daci," he murmured. "You're safe now."

With a little gasp, her eyes popped open. Those rich mocha depths and the small smile she offered were the most beautiful things he'd ever seen to date, bar none.

"Sorry I wimped out on you," she whispered.

"*Wimp* is never how I'd describe you."

Their hands met and clasped. Electricity was invented for that moment.

A throat cleared behind them. With an inner pang, Jax broke the connection, released her hand and turned toward Daci's brother. Noah's brown gaze held none of his sister's warmth, but it wasn't chilly, either. More like coolly speculative.

Jax drew himself up tall, meeting the assessment with a cool gaze of his own. He'd need time and quiet space to examine what had just passed between him and Daci, to know what it meant. But he wasn't about to let anyone else see how shaken he was by a simple look and meeting of the hands. More so even than being shot at and chased.

"Know any doctors who do house calls?" he managed in calm tones.

"On the way."

Daci murmured her brother's name. Noah brushed past Jax and took a seat on the edge of the bed.

"Hey, Mamasis. Welcome home. You look like something the cat dragged in and smell like you've been crawling through a sewer."

The brotherly teasing drew a grin onto Daci's face.

Jax let out a chuckle and sniffed at his own clothes. "This sewer cat needs to find the officer in charge around here, get a status update and ask someone to retrieve our luggage from my wrecked car. Then I'm all for a shower."

"And a little antiseptic for that cut on your ear." Noah swiveled toward him. "Thanks for saving my sister. Again." There was no reservation in the sincerity written on his face.

Jax nodded. "My pleasure."

There was no reservation in his sincerity, either. Sure, he'd go to the mat to defend any helpless human being. It's what he did daily—though not usually with bullets flying. At least not since he'd quit the Marshals Service. But this ferocity over Daci's well-being was far beyond the everyday passion of his calling. This was something else. Something more. Something he hadn't felt since Regan. And that's what terrified him.

If he had begun to love Candace Marlowe the way he'd loved Regan, how could he bear that kind pain all over again if this madman who was after her achieved his goal? But regardless of his heart's peril, he had to keep his head in the game and make sure that didn't happen. Only after this vendetta was stopped and the perp was in custody could he take the time to figure out his feelings and if she reciprocated them, because right now emotions were irrelevant.

* * *

Two mornings later, a conclave of law-enforcement personnel sat around a massive mahogany table in the mansion's formal dining room. Daci occupied the seat at the head of the table, still wearing loose-fitting clothing but looking bright eyed and with good color in her face. Jax flanked her on her right and Noah on her left. He was the only civilian in the bunch, but since he'd need to be in on what was being planned, Daci had insisted on his presence and met little resistance from the PD or the Marshals Service.

DC Bartlett from the Boston office of the Marshals Service stood at the foot of the table. The man's craggy face wore what Jax could only call a triumphant smirk. The man clapped square hands together, and conversation ceased as all eyes turned toward him.

"We've received a piece of good news—not just for Deputy Marlowe's present safety, but for many others who might have been targeted through this man's services. The person calling himself The Connection has been identified and taken into custody."

A cheer swept around the table.

"Who is it?" Daci asked.

The DC's expression sobered. "The same person your IT system clue led us to arrest.

Unfortunately, he has lawyered up and isn't talking, so we're still digging the old-fashioned way to expose his double-dealings."

Jax drew in a breath. The mole in the Marshals Service had not only been selling inside information, but brokering hits, too. Quite a coup to bring the pariah to justice. Quite a black eye that the traitor was unearthed within their own system.

"Springfield or Boston?" Jax asked.

"Boston," the DC answered. "Interestingly enough, HQ hired the guy away from the Boston PD about a year after your carjacking. In one of your reports, Deputy Marlowe, you said you were looking for an explanation why Samuel Clayhorn's mug shot wasn't among those presented to you when your grandmother was killed. We think this guy was on the take back then, too. Probably got paid to yank the photo."

Jax locked gazes with Daci. She offered a small nod with the barest hint of a smile. At least the culprit wasn't Randy from the Springfield office.

"Why is this such good news?" Noah asked.

Daci touched his arm. "This Connection creepazoid is the one who was brokering the bounty on me on behalf of whoever wants me dead. With the broker apprehended, the hitters will stop coming, because they have no chance of getting paid."

A smile bloomed across her brother's face. "You're home free?"

"Not exactly," Jax said. "The person who contracted the hit is still out there, but we've bought some time, because it should take him or her a while to find another broker, or a new way to get to Daci."

Noah scowled. "What are we going to do about that?"

"I have an idea," Daci announced with an inquiring look toward the DC.

Brow furrowed, the man settled into a chair. "I suggest you share it."

"Jax and I have discussed this." She folded her fingers over his on the table. "But we kept the idea to ourselves because of the mole issue that's just been resolved."

Jax was tempted to jerk his hand away because he still hated her auction idea. Unbelievably risky. But he hated remaining on the defensive even worse. As she explained, Jax's gaze met Noah's and found a reflection of his own conflicted opinion there.

The PD and Marshals Service representatives expressed no such conflict—they were openly approving of the idea. Specifics were debated until the plan started to take shape.

Daci, along with Jax and Noah and any of her other siblings who could help, would spend the next three weeks handling arrangements for the auction. Meanwhile, all available law enforcement personnel would get out there turning over rocks in hopes of exposing the culprit. The case would be a priority right up there with tracking down Liggett Naylor.

"And finding Serena and Chase," Daci inserted.

Jax seconded the thought, but realistically understood the investigation into their disappearance had gone cold until new information surfaced. He prayed it would, for the child's sake. But even more intensely, he prayed that the commitment to protect one of their own would drive the law-enforcement community to lengths beyond heroic to find Daci's deadly enemy *before* she had to become bait at her own auction. Either way, whether the auction went forward or not, it would take a nuclear blast to remove him from her side until her would-be killer was brought to justice.

TEN

Seated in a soft chair in the sunroom, Daci frowned down at her colored pen creating designs in the leather-bound notebook Jax had given her. The journal, along with all of their personal items that had been in Jax's trashed car, had been retrieved by law enforcement the very day they'd run the gauntlet to the estate. In the two weeks since then, she'd added to her hospital-time doodles and made significant inroads on the pages, but not so much progress in coming up with theories or even ferreting out old memories that might lend a clue as to who was targeting her for death.

Even more disheartening, the PD investigation had confirmed her speculation that, at the time of her grandmother's murder by a carjacker, Uncle Conrad had been working at an illegal chop shop. He may even have provided information as to when and where Daci and her grandmother shopped so the jacker could come grab the car. Only the operation had turned out anything but quick and clean. She and Grandma Katie must have returned to the car sooner than anticipated, catching the thief in the act and rewarding Grandma with a bullet. Her uncle had been indirectly responsible for his mother's death. What a horrible betrayal of family ties, and what a burden to carry through life!

Little wonder he'd been a bitter man who pushed people away. Few would be fretting that the memorial service for him had been postponed until this matter of the attempts on her life was resolved.

"The furrows on the paper are almost as deep as the ones on your brow."

Daci jumped at Jax's voice, and a pang shot through her middle. Her physical recovery was progressing nicely, but quick movements still brought pain.

"You startled me!"

"Sorry." Jax settled onto the settee opposite her.

He looked positively delicious in blue jeans and a pale green polo shirt smudged with the dust and sweat of strenuous activity. This hopeless attraction to him was another thing she couldn't seem to resolve. Through her internet discoveries while she was in the hospital, she understood why, for him, a romance with someone in law enforcement would be taboo—way too emotionally wrenching. And she did, indeed, plan to return to the Marshals Service as soon as her would-be killer had been caught. She'd been in love with the idea of helping and protecting others for as long as she could remember.

Jax leaned toward her, elbows on his knees. "Nate and I have finished sorting through the old carriage house, and we need you to come put your stamp of approval on potential auction items."

Noah had gone out on assignment yesterday, and Nate had shown up for duty this morning.

Daci smiled and laid her notebook and pen on a side table. "Sounds a lot simpler than brainstorming against a blank wall."

"Still baffled about the person behind the hit on you?"

"You got it."

"Frustrating!"

"Tell me about it."

Jax rose and held out his hand. She took it, reveling in the strength of the fingers wrapped around hers, as he helped her to stand. Physical weakness was the other frustration she faced daily, but the doctor kept assuring her that she'd fully recover—eventually. The process was much too slow to suit her, especially right now.

As soon as she was on her feet, Daci disengaged her hand from Jax's. She instantly missed the touch, but restoring professional distance was for the best. He offered a lopsided smile, but his eyes were sad, as if he understood her reasoning and regretted it, too.

They went out the glass door into the sunshine and crossed the lawn toward the carriage house. The detritus of centuries had accumulated in that building and in the attic of the main house, which had already been scoured for trash and treasures. Anything that fit the former category had met its fate in the Dumpster; much of the latter had been tagged for auction.

Even though Daci hadn't been in on the physical labor, a sense of accomplishment filled her. From the attic, items of small intrinsic value but great historical value had been donated to museums; items of great intrinsic value but small sentimental value had been tagged for sale, and items with great sentimental value—which were few—had been brought out of storage and displayed in the house where family could enjoy them.

Now, the same process was taking place in the spacious early-1700s building that used to house several carriages, horses and staff. Since the early twentieth century, the building had become a garage down below and a junk repository in the second-floor living quarters. Sometime during the transition from horse and buggy to horseless carriage, it had become a Marlowe family tradition to hire a couple who became housekeeper and chauffeur and lived in the pool house, rather than the carriage house. At the moment, neither lived on-site, and Daci had no plans to ever hire a chauffeur, so Jax occupied the pool house.

She and Jax stepped through the door of the garage and nearly collided with Nate. Her brother halted with this odd twinkle in his gaze as he looked from one to the other of them. Daci narrowed her eyes. The twins were up to something, or else they had the wrong idea about her and Jax. Before he left on assignment, Noah had been looking at them like that, too.

"I'll go whip us up some burgers," her brother said. "My gut needs grub. Come on back to the kitchen when you're finished here, and I'll have dinner on."

"Sounds great. Will do." Jax stepped aside for Nate.

Daci peeked her head out the door and watched her brother stride across the lawn, whistling. The housekeeping and lawn-care services they employed were day workers. Events like the upcoming auction were catered, but for the most part, this generation of Marlowes preferred to look after their own basic needs like cooking personal meals, doing their own laundry and cleaning their rooms. At least, that's the way she'd brought them up, and none of them complained. Well, not anymore. She was desperately proud of them all.

"You have a lot to be proud of in them," Jax said, as if hearing her thoughts.

He seemed to read her well quite often. The habit was disconcerting and gratifying at the same time.

She turned toward him with a smile. "What have you got to show me?

Jax started toward the interior stairs at the far side of the garage area. Daci followed, but her leg brushed against the Lexus's bumper, a car she'd never driven since the day the carjacking had happened, but hadn't had the heart to sell. She stopped with her hand on the fancy silver vehicle's hood, eyes squeezed tightly closed. Fear-soaked memory swept through her—a wild-eyed man wielding a gun, the sharp report of a shot, the shock on her grandmother's face as a blood rose erupted from her chest and she crumpled to the tarmac.

A whimper left Daci's throat, and, moments later, strong arms enfolded her. She buried her head against Jax's chest as tears came. What was the matter with her? She hadn't fallen apart like this over that long-ago event since shortly after it happened. Being wounded by a bullet herself must have unlocked reservoirs of that deep hurt.

"It's okay to feel," Jax murmured to her, his breath warm across her scalp. "Grief is like that. It jumps on you out of nowhere—even years later. Believe me, I know."

Daci hiccuped and sniffled and pulled back from Jax's embrace, wiping her hands across her wet cheeks. "Thanks. I know you know. I admire how you've gone on with a productive life."

"Productive? I aim for that. Lonely? I *don't* aim for that, but I've hit the mark anyway."

Daci blinked up at the chiseled face that had softened into vulnerability.

"I can't stop blaming myself." His eyes went wide, and the words blurted from his mouth as if he wanted to stop them but couldn't.

"Why do you blame yourself?"

Jax turned away and leaned back against the Lexus. "My pregnant wife was riding with me in a Marshals Service vehicle when some wacko who hated cops pulled up next to us at a stop sign and opened fire with an automatic weapon. If she hadn't been sitting between me and the shooter, I'd be the one dead, not her. Not my baby."

His legs seemed to give way, and he slid down the side of the Lexus to sit on the floor, hugging his knees. Ignoring twinges from her midsection, Daci sat down next to him. She wasn't going to let this opportunity to see into his heart slip by her.

"Then she'd be the one grieving *your* loss."

"Sure, but at least she'd have the baby. They both would have been well taken care of. I made those arrangements as soon as we were married."

"You're a conscientious person, but no one can anticipate the irrational actions of others."

"You don't understand." He glared at her, then went back to studying the garage floor. "She shouldn't have been with me in a federal vehicle. Even the tabloids said so."

"Right, the *tabloids*. None of the reputable news services hinted at such an unfair judgment. I read all the news stories regarding the incident. Your wife's car wouldn't start, and she was going to be late for her prenatal doctor's appointment. She called you to come get her. You were returning from a witness interview and were closer to your house than the office where you'd parked your personal vehicle, so you called in to request permission to pick your wife up in the work vehicle. DC Reynolds gave you that permission. Do you blame *him*, too?"

Jax stared at her as if she'd gone off her nut. "Of course not. He was doing me a favor."

"And you were doing your wife a favor in the best way you knew how."

He let out a bitter chuckle. "I know that up here." He tapped two fingers against the side of his head. "Can't figure out how to convince this." He put a hand over his heart.

"I guess I'll pray God helps that happen for you then."

"You're praying?" His gaze was a hopeful.

Face warming, she shrugged. "More than I had been since my grandma died. I've come to realize she'd want me to and that God's been waiting for me to be ready to break the silence. Thank you for nudging me in the right direction. Hearing you talk about your faith after what you've suffered sort of wised me up."

"You're welcome. And thank you for listening to me and *not* agreeing with the tabloids."

"That's what friends are for."

His gaze went shuttered, and he turned his head away. "Yeah, friends."

Awkward silence fell.

Daci studied the laces of her sneakers. He'd said the word "friend" like it wasn't exactly his favorite. Had she misspoken? Wasn't that the most either of them could ask for from the other? But what if it wasn't? What if he wanted more? Could she go there? Could *he*? Judging by what he'd been telling her about the state of his heart after the loss of his wife, the answer was no. Not now. Maybe not ever. Best they remain nothing more than friends, as difficult as that might be when she could so easily fall for this guy.

"What sort of mess did you run into up there?" She pointed over their heads.

"Come and see." Resurrecting his lost grin, Jax stood up and helped her to her feet for the second time that day.

They trooped upstairs into the long-neglected, apartment-style dwelling, arriving in what was once a sitting room and was now stuffed with several stacks of boxes full of who-knew-what and articles of ancient furniture. Noah and Jax had opened a few windows, so much of the musty smell had blown away, but a trace lingered, tickling Daci's nostrils.

Jax motioned at the conglomeration. "This is stuff Nate deemed best suited for the auction. We have a number of pieces of antique furniture that should clean up nicely, and the boxes hold a variety of silver services that need polishing, seventeenth-and eighteenth-century china tableware and figurines, and odd collectible items, as well as some original artwork your brother didn't think your family would care to keep."

Daci nodded. "I trust his judgment. Besides, if we haven't missed any of this stuff all of our lives, we certainly don't need it now. The Uniquely Made Foundation needs the proceeds more."

"You don't care to go through the stuff?"

"Why bother? I'll see it tomorrow when the appraiser comes in to evaluate it. I'm more interested in what Nate wants to us keep. In our family, he's the most inclined to pack-rat-itis."

Jax laughed. "Okay. That kind of thing is in what used to be the main bedroom. We didn't touch the items in the back bedroom."

"Why not?"

"Nate said it was your parents' personal things. He seemed a little skittish about digging through those boxes."

Daci's mouth went dry. The day after her parents' funeral, she and her grandmother had gone through the house to root out and destroy any alcohol, drugs or paraphernalia. Then, exhausted physically and emotionally, Grandma had hired a couple of temporary workers to put her daughter and son-in-law's personal belongings into boxes and store the things away up here. At the time, Daci promised herself to go through things someday. What better "someday" than right now when they were in the swing of sorting and throwing?

"I want to start there," Daci announced.

"Are you sure you're up to it?"

Daci snorted. "I've been sitting around like a wallflower for two weeks. A little activity isn't going to hurt me. I promise not to lift anything. Why don't you bring me one of those burgers Nate's making, and I'll get started."

"I can see you're not going to be talked out of this, but behave yourself while I'm gone." He shook a finger at her. "I'll be back as quickly as I can to do any grunt work."

"Yes, Papa." Daci laughed and headed toward the back of the apartment.

The musty smell grew decidedly stronger, and she decided to get professional housecleaners up here to give the place a full scrub as soon as all the stored items were removed. Even if they didn't really use this space, they still had an obligation to maintain it properly.

At the closed door of the room that held the personal belongings of parents she'd loved but had never been able to respect, she paused with her hand on the antique glass knob.

"Here goes," she whispered to herself. "You can do this."

Twenty minutes after she'd entered the room, she perched on the edge of a cedar chest, hugging herself and trying to stop shaking. Her world had come crashing in on itself once again.

Pleased that he'd remembered before Nate had to remind him that Daci liked a few pickled jalapeños on her burger, Jax trotted up the steps in the carriage house. A large serving tray held two high-end paper plates—if such things could be dubbed high-end—that sported fat, juicy burgers, deli potato salad, carrot sticks and a couple of bottles of water. If Daci was going to attempt physical labor, he'd make sure she was hydrated.

At the top of the stairs, he stopped to listen. The place was suspiciously quiet. Then a soft sob broke the silence. Had she fallen and hurt herself? Heart rate rocketing, Jax plopped the tray onto the nearest box top and took off for the back room. He found Daci slumped atop a wooden chest, rocking back and forth and hugging something tight against her torso.

Jax hit his knees. "What happened? Are you hurt?"

She shook her head, sniffling deeply. "Not

physically. There are…worse ways of being hurt." The words came out waterlogged and ragged.

Daci loosened her grip on the object she held and let it flop onto her lap. It was a small sketch pad.

"One of your parents was a doodler, too?" Jax struggled to comprehend what might be going on.

"My mother." Daci sat up straight. "But not a doodler. A real artist, especially in drawing people. She never used her talent except to amuse herself, which was truly the world's loss. I found this pad and quite a few others in this chest. The date on the cover made it the last one she'd been working in before she and my dad were murdered. Naturally, I was curious and—" Her voice broke.

Without another word, she handed Jax the pad. Gut hollow, he opened to the first page and found a sketch of a man's face. Every stroke of the pencil contributed to forming such a detailed likeness it could almost have been a black-and-white photograph. The man was handsome and laughing, but lines of dissipation around his eyes, nose and mouth and an infinite emptiness in the eyes, created a wrenching impact of sadness rather than joy.

"My father," Daci said. "Go on until you reach the last sketch."

Slowly Jax paged through more drawings, mostly of people at parties or dining or shopping. Probably the stuff of the artist's everyday life. There were a few of the Marlowe children, including Daci as a teenager. Those he would have liked to linger over—so vivid, so revealing of character—but she urged him onward.

At last, he reached an up-close facial sketch that stopped him cold. He looked up and met Daci's stricken gaze.

"What is a drawing of a young Liggett Naylor doing in your mother's sketch pad?"

"Read the notation on the bottom."

Jax returned his gaze to the drawing. Most of the renderings in the book hadn't included a caption or even a signature, but sure enough, in the right-hand corner, where an artist's signature might go, plain block letters read, "Niall's father."

Jax gulped against a tightness in his throat. "Niall? Your youngest brother who was born with FAS?"

"A quirky thing about my mother. When pregnant the first four times, she managed to lay off the sauce, allowing us to enter the world healthy. Not so with her last pregnancy. It was as if she didn't care."

Daci continued to tremble, and Jax laid a comforting hand on her knee.

"I was only ten years old when he was born," she continued. "I got to hold him once at the hospital. Grandmother brought me to visit. From the moment I cuddled him, I loved Niall with all of my heart. I could see he wasn't quite normal, and my brain was spinning with plans about how to take care of him and protect him, but I never got the chance. My dad brought my mom home, but not Niall. In response to my nagging, my parents told me he was dead and buried and wouldn't discuss the matter further. Wouldn't even tell me where to find the grave. Lack of closure has haunted me all my life, but I never could have guessed this horrible secret."

She wrung her hands together. "Where did my mother meet Liggett Naylor? He's not the sort she would run into at a high-society bash. Did my mom have an affair? Was she raped? Did my dad know? Possibly not. If he knew my mom had been unfaithful to him, the subject would have come up—loudly—in one of their arguments. Our tender ears were never considered in the content of verbal battles."

In Jax's breast, deep anger warred with great sorrow. "You know we have to show this to

Rey. This is going to open up a whole other line of investigation."

"I know." She sighed. "I have a ton of questions that need answering. Having law-enforcement help to find those answers is probably for the best."

"Especially if this family connection to Naylor is behind the attempts on your life. It seems too coincidental that his escape from custody was followed by a hit contract on you."

"But why now—over two decades after his involvement with my mother? And why only come after me and not the rest of my family? Though I'm thankful for that little detail. I'd be going out of my skull if my siblings were being targeted."

"Hopefully, we'll find that out when we track Naylor down."

Within the hour, the revelation of Daci's family connection to Liggett Naylor had created a flurry of activity within both the PD and the Marshals Service. The old case file on her parents' murders was reopened. No one put it past Naylor to have been involved in their deaths. Perhaps that mass shooting wasn't so random after all. Had the man in prison for the crime been framed? Even though the party guest been found passed out from booze and drugs with the gun in his hand—open-and-shut case—maybe he hadn't pulled the trigger.

A couple of days later, Jax located Daci in the kitchen, sitting on a bar stool at the quartz-topped island. Her fork hovered over a plate of lasagna, but she was staring off into space. He didn't blame her for being preoccupied, not only with her shocking revelation, but with auction preparations. He'd been trying to talk her into postponing the charity function. What was the need for it right now if they'd identified who was after her?

He settled on the stool beside her, and she spared him a sober glance.

"Smells good." He gestured at her plate.

"There's lots left over from last night." She waved her fork at the refrigerator. "Never mind. You can have this." She slid her plate toward him. "I thought I was hungry, but I guess I'm not."

He slid the plate back to her. "Hungry or not, you need to eat. You've been picking at your food like a bird the past couple of days. That's no way to regain your strength."

"I appreciate your consideration, but physically, I've been feeling much improved. Mentally, I'm just boggled, and emotionally—well, you don't want to go there."

"Have you spoken to your siblings about your discovery?"

She wrinkled her nose in that adorable way of hers. "Yes, and they weren't pretty conversations. *Blown away* would be putting their reactions mildly. Nate didn't want to leave me to return to his practice, and the others wanted to rush back here. I've banned them from the premises. With Naylor in the picture, any place around me is too dangerous. He's got goons galore on his direct payroll. He doesn't have to waste time trying to locate a new hit broker."

Jax frowned. She had a point. "Then why did he go the hire-a-hit route in the first place?"

"I'm not sure he did. Maybe the person after me isn't Naylor after all. What if someone is trying to protect Naylor from whatever threat he or she thinks I pose? That's why we need to move ahead with the auction. Someone within my parents' set of acquaintances introduced Naylor into my mother's life. I've got a certainty in my gut that whoever it is will try for me then. Once we catch them, that could be the break we need to find out where Naylor is."

Jax had a certainty in his gut, too—whatever it took to ensure this threat to Daci was forever ended, he would do it. Yet a stray doubt niggled at him. What if he failed Daci like he'd failed Regan?

ELEVEN

All that glitters is most definitely not gold.
The cliché wandered through Daci's mind as she surveyed the vast third-floor ballroom of the Marlowe estate house. The thought had not come because of the costly items on display that would soon be auctioned off, but because of the people garbed in their glitzy best. Hardly anyone on the guest list had failed to put in an appearance, leaving the field wide open for who among them wanted her dead.

Dozens of Boston's upper crust, as well as many others who aspired to be accepted as such, flowed from item to item. The buzz of comments and conversation nearly drowned out the string quartet that provided background music for the gala event. The servers bearing hors d'oeuvres and designer non-alcoholic beverages on trays glided silently and nearly unnoticed through the crowd. The anonymity was a good thing, since every one of them was either a deputy marshal or a member of the police force.

Even Jax hadn't been able to say the law-enforcement coverage was inadequate. But she still had the impression he'd prefer her to be locked up in a tower until her hair grew long enough to reach the ground or her deadly enemy was exposed, whichever came first.

And there came Mr. Protective now, striding toward her in a tux and bow tie. A pleasant shiver swirled down Daci's spine. The man did clean up grand. Not that he'd been shabby in his lawyer suit, but she'd started to get used to him in jeans and a polo shirt covered in dust. To explain why a Springfield resident was attending this strictly Boston do, he had been introduced to guests as her boyfriend. His idea, not hers, but a stupid bit of her kept wishing the status was not a cover but the real thing. A lot of good wishing had ever done her.

Sorry, Lord. I promised to pray, not whine. I'll get back on that plan.

"Have I told you yet that you look stunning?" Jax took her hands in his and grinned down at her.

Her stomach did a flip, but she commanded the ornery organ into place and responded with a cool smile.

"Thank you, kind sir, but I could say, 'This old thing?' and mean it."

She glanced down at the art deco beaded sheath gown in silver-blue that she'd pulled out of her closet from a years-ago engagement party for a school friend. The current situation hadn't allowed her to go shopping for new clothes. She'd even done her hair herself in a partial updo that swept all but a few strands of strawberry blond curls away from her face and into a twisted gather high on the back of her head, leaving a generous waterfall flowing down her back.

"Here are the lovebirds," a female voice cooed.

Daci's heart jumped. She knew that voice. Felicity Horner, one of her best friends from high school—the one for whose party she'd worn this dress. If Daci was worried about keeping up social appearances, she might have been embarrassed about re-wearing the dress, but sadness was all she really felt. Maybe a little guilt, too. She hadn't stayed close with any of her high school friends—mostly because the majority had gone off to college while she stayed home to look after her siblings.

"Fliss!" Daci turned to find her old friend gazing at her with speculative hazel eyes. "It's good to see you." She hugged the other woman and received an air kiss in return. "I must have been AWOL from my greeting post when you arrived."

"No problem. Your hunk of a boyfriend made me feel welcome." Felicity sent Jax a coy smile.

He offered a small bow. "Glad you could attend tonight. I'll leave you two to catch up while I do some more mingling."

Daci's gaze followed Jax's easy stride until he melted into the swelling crowd. Of course, Felicity's gaze did the same. The woman's expression could only be described as predatory. Daci resisted the impulse to form claws with her fingers. What did it say about her that she reacted so strongly to someone's interest in a man who was only *posing* as her boyfriend?

Daci commanded herself to stand down. She wasn't entirely clueless about the events in her old friend's life since they'd last been in touch. Over the past weeks, the Marshals Service had conducted deep background checks into all of Daci's proposed guests. It had felt a little uncomfortable reading details about the lives of old friends and acquaintances—including facts that weren't publicly known and that the guests had, in fact, taken great pains to hide— but she had to study the reports to see if anything jumped out at her as to who might want to kill her. Nothing had, but she came to the party armed with a lot of catch-up information on her former friends, as well as friends of her parents.

Felicity's first marriage had fallen apart within a few years. Now the woman was in the midst of divorcing her third husband and taking him to the cleaners like she'd done the others. If the jaded expression in Felicity's eyes said anything, she hadn't found happiness or fulfillment in her wealth or her multiple attempts at love, only bitterness.

The woman swiveled and faced Daci. "You look surprisingly good, Dace. I mean, I *heard* about you getting shot. Why on earth have you gone into such a dangerous profession? Why go into any profession at all when you have this?" She followed the questions with a brief laugh and a wave around the room.

Daci smiled and shook her head. "You were always direct. Glad to see that hasn't changed. To tell you the truth, by the time my sibs hopped off my plate and into the wide world, I was a challenge junkie. I had to get busy with something that keeps me on my toes."

"And you've always been one driven to right the wrongs of this world." Felicity's tone was a bit condescending and her smile brittle, as if she considered it naive of Daci to think good might triumph over evil.

Daci's heart broke for her old friend. Hoping to lighten the tone, she redirected the conversation. "Is your dad here, too?"

Griffin Horner was one of the suspects high on her list. The Horner family had been frequent guests at the Marlowe estate for generations. Griffin had become her parents' best party buddy, and should have been at the bash where they'd been massacred, but a case of the flu—or so he'd claimed at the time—had kept him home that evening. The current background check revealed he'd lost his taste for the high life after that shocking event, and displaying a knack for arbitrage, entered the family banking business.

"No, Daddy is out of the country attending a bunch of dry financial meetings." Felicity tossed a lock of her chocolate-brown hair over her shoulder. "I rarely see him anymore, but Grandfather is here." She waved manicured fingernails toward a small group chatting near the display of a century-old silver service.

Gerald Horner leaned on a gold-handled cane as he sipped from a fluted glass. He had always been a slight man, and his stature had diminished over time, leaving him resembling a lad sporting a tuxedo at a junior high party…until one saw his deeply lined face and the shrewd eyes he now turned on his grand-daughter and her friend. One hand lifted in acknowledgment of their attention, then he turned toward someone who was speaking to him.

"Where are Nate and Noah, Am and Ava?" Felicity reclaimed Daci's focus.

Daci could hardly say she'd forbidden her brothers and sisters from attending the auc-tion for their own safety, but she'd prepared a little speech. "Their lives are so busy. I don't think they'll be able to—"

"There they are!" Felicity flapped a hand toward the ballroom entrance.

Stomach clenching, Daci turned to find her siblings parading into the party in full dress regalia. Her heart swelled even as it sank. They looked so good, she had to be proud; they'd disobeyed her wishes, and she had to be mad. As if they'd felt her laser vision zeroed in on them—which, from long experience, they probably had—their heads turned toward her almost as one. She glared, but they all grinned and fluttered their fingers at her.

Felicity gripped Daci's arm. "Nate and Noah have grown into absolute dishes! They *were* only four years younger than us, right? I'm going to go renew acquaintance. Talk to you later, Dace."

The woman swept off toward her prey. Daci hid a shark smile. Over the years, her twin brothers had grown expert at foiling the wiles of man-eaters far more cunning than Fliss. They'd be fine. They'd also be distracted from watchdogging their older sister, which suited Daci perfectly.

A throat clearing behind her brought Daci's attention around to find Felicity's grandfather smiling up at her. "Wonderful idea—this auction. Excellent turnout." His gaze swept the room, then returned to her. "I was wondering if I might speak to you privately in the small library before the auction begins."

Daci's pulse sped up. Was this the moment they'd prepared for, when someone would try to get her alone? But this was *Gerald* Horner, the grand old man her parents had always called "stuffy and boring." She couldn't fathom the idea of him overseeing a chain of chop shops to line his pockets. But forget indulging in amazement. It was time to play along. Maybe—finally—find out what the attempts on her life had been all about.

"Certainly." Daci nodded.

"After you." He gestured toward the main doors with his cane.

Skin prickling, Daci preceded her guest out of the cavernous ballroom, hyperaware of the many pairs of guardian eyes that were watching. The microphone embedded in the sapphire-and-diamond necklace at her throat suddenly seemed hot against her skin, and the small pistol strapped to her calf managed to abruptly grow pounds heavier. But despite the tension, she also felt alert, primed for danger.

She was ready. Let the show begin.

Out of the press of guests, Daci waited for Gerald to come up beside her at the top of the stairs. She preferred them to descend in tandem. Being pushed down the steps by someone behind her didn't sound appealing, though such a blatant ploy seemed unlikely.

The older man joined her with a smile that appeared anything but sinister. All of her seeing-behind-the-outward-expression experience read genuine warmth. Maybe this wasn't a trick with deadly motive. If not, she still needed to be ultracareful, because whoever wanted her dead might take advantage of her time away from the crowd. Fliss's grandfather may have unwittingly put himself in danger as collateral damage.

Great! Now she needed to protect him as well as herself.

The older man took each stair slowly, gripping the railing with one hand and using his cane to support his other side. Daci resisted the urge to offer her arm. She had the sense her guest would be insulted. Besides, physical contact with someone who *might* want to kill her didn't seem wise.

Eventually, they reached the second floor, and Daci guided Gerald up the hallway to the small study/library that was adjacent to what had been her parents' master bedroom. Ever since she was a child, Daci had loved to come here, surrounded by the smell of books, and nestle onto the seat set into the bay window with a mug of cocoa and a novel. When she needed a haven away from rowdy siblings or arguing parents, she could pull the thick, velvet curtains closed over the window seat and feel safe from the world. The safety was an illusion, of course, but a handy one for preserving sanity at the time.

Daci crossed the room and took a position behind the desk only a few feet from her favorite spot. Gerald stopped in front of the desk.

"How can I help you?" she asked.

The man's gaze lowered toward his feet, and he seemed to shrink smaller. "Please forgive us."

"Forgive you for what?" Daci's skin crawled. Her mind's eye played with a scenario where he yanked a pistol from his waistband and said, *For killing you,* as he pulled the trigger. Daci scolded her ripe imagination as the older man wrung his hands together and refused to meet her gaze.

"Before Griffin left for Europe, he shared some disturbing information with me about his youthful escapades, and I must apologize for our part in—"

At the sound of a soft swish like a curtain parting, Gerald's head jerked up. His eyes flew wide on a spot beyond Daci's shoulder.

"What are *you* doing here?" he cried as Daci whirled toward the window seat.

A startled cry came from within the library, and Jax left off lurking outside the door and charged into the room. Daci struggled with a tuxedo-clad male attempting to plunge the needle of a syringe into her neck. Jax sprang toward the fray, but the small man in front of the desk thrust his stick in front of his legs, tripping him to the floor. Nose burning from carpet contact, Jax rolled onto his back and barely got an arm in front of his face as the stick whipped down.

Crack! Pain burst through his wrist.

A scream from Daci energized him, and with his right hand he caught the cane that was again descending toward him and shoved. The man he recognized as Gerald Horner from the reports he and Daci had studied prior to this event tottered backward and plopped down onto his backside.

Jax surged to his feet, holding his injured left arm close to his body, and rammed his shoulder into Daci's assailant. The man staggered sideways. In one graceful movement, Daci bent, swept her gown away from her leg and pulled out a .22 pistol.

She pointed it at the man with the syringe. "Stop right there."

By the "I mean business" tone in her voice and the look in her eyes, if Jax had been standing in front of that pistol, he'd have frozen on the spot. But desperation twisted the stranger's doughy face, and he lifted the syringe as if he would throw it at her like a dart. The .22 spoke, the syringe shattered, and the man screamed.

"You have to die!" he wailed, clutching a bleeding hand to his chest. "You can't live, or our family is ruined!"

"Griffin Horner, why are you trying to kill me?" Daci asked.

"Yes, Griff, what do you think you're doing?" snapped Gerald. He sat in a heap on the floor, staring toward Daci's assailant.

"We all want answers to those questions,"

said Rey as he led a group of deputy marshals into the room.

"This is your fault, Dad," Griffin spit out as a deputy cuffed him.

"My fault!" the father protested as he was helped to his feet by a pair of deputies. "Have you gone insane? Think what your behavior is going to do to our reputation. I was more than happy to do as you asked and invite Candace into the small library to apologize on behalf of our family for your poor choices that contributed to Candace's parents' profligate lifestyle, but I had no idea you were setting up an ambush."

"Hold it!" Jax interrupted. "Why did you hit me with your cane if you weren't in on the murder plot?"

The elderly man lifted his chin and sniffed. "You were about to attack my son. I did what any father would do."

"Even if that son was trying to kill someone?"

"Horners stick together." He straightened his suit jacket. "We have our honor to think about."

Griffin snorted. "You can stop blathering about family honor. You trashed that long ago, Dad." He pronounced the title with a sneer. "Your nose is stuck so high in the air you have no idea what your old indiscretions have produced. We're reaping the consequences of one of them today. We are ruined in Boston society as soon as people find out."

"I have no idea what you're talking about," Gerald said, but his tone was less than certain.

"Me, either," Daci said.

Griffin glared at Daci. "Don't play innocent with me, missy. He told me you knew about the connection between him and us. He said your uncle tried to use that to get out of being shot, claiming that if he turned up dead, you'd know where to find his killer."

Daci looked blank, but a bunch of tumblers clicked into place for Jax.

"You're talking about Liggett Naylor."

The younger Horner's mouth pursed like he'd sucked on a dill pickle, but he said nothing.

Daci crossed her arms. "Uncle Conrad never mentioned to me any connection between your family and Liggett Naylor. However, you're too late if you were trying to stop me from finding out that Naylor was my baby brother's father. What in the world would that have to do with *you*?"

"This isn't about *your* brother—it's about mine. The one Dad never knew about or acknowledged."

Jax's gut went hollow. "Liggett Naylor is your brother?"

"Half, if you don't mind. I'm the one who introduced him to Daci's mother. I was young. Wild. Stupid. At first, Naylor was just the low-life who hooked us up with the best hooch for the parties. It wasn't until we were deep into that sort of business relationship that he informed me we were related. Had proof even. He got my DNA at one of our parties and had it compared to his. Remember Vivian Naylor, Dad? The fling you had so long ago?"

The older man turned red and began spluttering and protesting.

Rey hushed him up with a word, then turned toward Griffin. "I get the idea you know where Naylor is. Spit it out."

The man wriggled, clearly torn. He was probably scared of what his half brother would do to him in retaliation. On the other hand, the dark looks all the law enforcement officers were giving him had Griffin visibly nervous. "You have to understand. He's been holding the past over my head for years. What would people say when they found out my father sired a mass murderer? When he escaped, he made me provide him a safe house."

Jax stepped squarely into Griffin's personal space. "Where—is—he?"

For a bare second, the man glared at Jax, then he wilted. "My pool house."

"Are a young woman and a baby with him?" Daci asked.

Griffin blinked at her. "No. He's alone with his remote control…except when he's out and about in one of my vehicles killing people like your uncle who was trying to shake him down and some guy he said panicked and attempted a clumsy hit-and-run. He called them both 'liabilities who knew too much,' so they had to go."

"I think Naylor is the one who killed my parents, not the man serving life without parole," Daci said.

"I think he did, too," Griffin agreed. "He saw your mom's sketchbook one day. That was the first he realized he'd fathered your youngest brother—the one who had been born not right and got shunted off to some institution. He was furious!"

Daci gasped. "Niall's not dead? Are you sure? Do you know where he is?"

Griffin shook his head. "Sorry."

Daci's shoulders slumped, and Jax put his good arm around her. She leaned into him, exactly the response he craved. Who was he fooling with his reasons for holding her at arm's length? The Lord had preserved her through so much. He needed to trust her life to Him, not his own feeble efforts. This woman was a treasure, and he'd be a prize idiot not to take a chance on love again. There was only one hitch—persuading her to feel the same way.

TWELVE

Saturday afternoon, a week after the Horner family's world imploded, Daci ran her fingers down the sleeve of the deputy marshal's uniform hanging in the closet of her duplex in Springfield. The doctor had cleared her to return to work on Monday. She grinned, but then her smile faded. Jax wouldn't be there. Her hand fell to her side.

Now that Naylor was in custody, their job together was over, their partnership ended. By now, Jax would be back fully into the groove of his chosen profession—protecting helpless innocents in the courtroom. She hadn't seen him since they'd wrapped up their final reports together a couple of days after the auction. He'd been in a cast from a cracked wrist.

"For a little old guy, Horner packed a wallop," Jax had told her with a grin.

He'd also sported a fresh scab on the end of his nose from a rug burn. It had taken all of Daci's self-control not to throw her arms around him and kiss the injured beak. But that would have been unprofessional. He'd made it clear any number of times that their relationship needed to remain at friendly colleague level. She had to respect his wishes, but— oh!—she wanted more.

"Stop pining for what isn't to be," she lectured herself out loud. "At least no one is still trying to kill you. Be thankful!"

Griffin Horner was being charged with harboring a fugitive, as well as conspiracy to commit murder, along with every suspected hitman in custody in connection with him posting a bounty on her life. Gerald faced charges of assaulting a deputy marshal.

Daci had tried to contact Felicity to say how sorry she was about this tragedy in her family, but Fliss wouldn't take her call. Probably for the best. She wasn't sure the Marshals Service would approve of the contact, and their friendship had been dead for years anyway. Whatever happened to the hopes and dreams Fliss had talked about when they were young? How terminally sad!

One very bright spot in the whole mess had put a figurative gold star in her service jacket—her contribution to the apprehension of Liggett Naylor. For all the blood and grief

Naylor's escape from custody had caused, his return to custody went without incident. While Daci was being debriefed by DC Reynolds, and her siblings were representing the family at the auction that continued uninterrupted, and Jax was being treated at the hospital ER, a team from the Boston office of the Marshals Service burst in on the escaped felon watching TV in Griffin Horner's pool house. Not a shot was fired.

Professionally, the only piece of the case that continued unsolved was the whereabouts of Serena and her baby. Daci would work on that when she returned to the office. Personally, two mysteries remained—who had left the basket of spoiled baby items on her front porch and the whereabouts of her brother, Niall. Both of those mysteries looked like they might never be solved.

The chime of her front doorbell shook Daci from her thoughts. She went to the door and checked the peephole. Her heart leaped, and she flung the door wide.

"Jaxon Williams! To what do I owe the pleasure?" Hopefully, her jaunty greeting hid the longing she felt in every cell of her being.

Since this was a weekend, he was clad in jeans and a polo shirt. His arm wore a cast, but he must have tossed his sling aside. She bit back a mamasis-style scold. At least the rug burn on his nose had faded significantly.

With an answering grin, he stepped inside. "I thought you might want to know Serena and Chase turned up this morning. They're both fine."

"What?" Daci pressed a hand to her chest. "Where have they been?"

A part of her did a happy dance that the pair were okay. Another part withered a little that Jax's visit was only on account of unfinished business. Or was it? If he had no interest in her beyond their temporary partnership, he could have phoned with the news. A tiny bud of hope began to unfurl in her heart.

"New York," he answered. "Apparently, she has a cousin in the Bronx no one knew about. That shooting incident at the park was the last straw for her after the attempted abduction. She called the cousin, and he was willing to take them in until it was safe to come home."

"What a relief they're all right!" Daci led her guest into the living room, and they took seats on easy chairs adjacent to each other. "Last Wednesday, I observed a police interview with Naylor through the two-way glass, and he continued to deny any involvement with their disappearance. I believed him, but that left us at square one in finding her and the baby. How is the little guy, by the way?"

"I have to admit I'm amazed at how well he's doing." Jax laughed. "I was called in this morning to attend the medical assessment, and he appears to be thriving and has clearly attached to his mother. Since that fact was so evident, and since his FAS condition makes him particularly fragile, the social worker reluctantly fell in with my recommendation that he remain with her until any consequences for her disappearance are determined. The danger to her and her child was so compelling that I believe the judge will be lenient. Especially since she had good reason not to turn to law enforcement—she knew better than anyone that the mole could lead Naylor straight to her."

Daci pursed her lips then nodded. "I'll be praying for them. In the meantime, maybe you can refer her to one of the Uniquely Made groups that are being formed. I wouldn't be surprised if she finds among them the wholesome, supportive friendships she needs."

"Good idea. I heard through the grapevine that the auction was a tremendous success. Congratulations! Your foundation will be able to fund a lot of new groups." Jax's expression sobered. "Did Naylor say anything about your parents?"

Emotion choked her, and she looked away. "He admitted to killing them," she finally managed.

Clearing her throat, she returned her attention to Jax. "Since he's already in for multiple life sentences without chance for parole, he had nothing to lose by telling the truth. Apparently, he found it quite the rush to massacre everyone at that party and pin it on the guest passed out in the corner." She hauled in a deep breath and let it out slowly. "At least, now an innocent man will be freed from prison."

Jax reached over and took her hand. "I'm sorry you had to hear something so horrible without anyone there to support you. If you had called me, I would have been there for you."

"You would?" Her fingers involuntarily closed around his.

"Always."

Daci's eyes widened at the intensity in his gaze. "Really?" The word came out a squeak.

"Absolutely. Daci, I— Well, would you consider— I mean, I'd like us to—"

A sudden tattoo of footsteps on the porch boards interrupted Jax's stammering. They both stiffened. Daci got up, and Jax followed on her heels. She peered through the peephole.

"No one is there," she told Jax.

"At least no one standing in front of the peep," he added.

"I'm going to look outside."

"I'm right behind you."

"Check."

She pulled the inner door open and the wider view through the screen door showed an empty porch. Almost empty anyway. Another basket sat at her feet. From what she could make out, it contained more baby items that were no doubt as rotten as the first ones. A sharp sound from the neighboring house signified its screen door banging shut. A hint of comprehension quivered through Daci.

Jax pulled out his cell and started pecking. "I'm calling the police."

Daci wrapped her hand around the phone, stopping him. "There's no threat in this strange gift. I think one of the residents next door is trying to get my attention. Let's go see."

Without waiting for agreement, she stepped outside. An odd sense of anticipation filled her as she picked up the basket by its handle and headed for the group home. Jax caught up with her within a few strides, and she offered him a reassuring smile. His answering scowl said he wasn't convinced this was a good idea.

The worker on duty let them in, and they found the residents enjoying a snack in the kitchen. A chorus of greetings welcomed them. The resident she'd never met before, only heard about as an autistic computer savant, appeared to be winded slightly from recent exertion. At sight of the basket, the young woman turned beet red, confirming Daci's suspicion.

"I believe you left this for me," she said in a gentle tone. "Your name is Paige. Right? Would you mind if we talked in private for a little while?"

Without meeting her gaze, the young woman nodded slowly and accompanied them into the living room. They all sat down, and Paige turned wary eyes on the basket Daci placed on the coffee table between them.

"Don't worry," Daci said to her. "You're not in trouble."

"You're not going to arrest me for stealing things from Jewel's sister's diaper bag?"

"I don't think an arrest is likely to happen." Jax's tone was stern. "But you did scare Daci."

Daci turned her head toward him. "It's okay, Jax. I just want to find out what is motivating the behavior." Her attention shifted to Paige. "I think you're angry with me for some reason that has to do with babies."

The young woman nodded, lowering her gaze to her hands folded in her lap.

"Could you explain to me *why* you're angry?" Keeping her tone soft and soothing was a struggle against the excitement growing within her.

Paige's hot and wounded gaze flickered to hers and then fell away. "When the others told me about our new neighbor, I recognized your name right away. I know what you did. You took care of the others, but you sent *him* away. You hurt him very much."

"Who?" Jax burst out.

Scarcely daring to breath, Daci placed a cautioning hand over his. "Yes, who did I send away?"

"My friend. He knows who you are. I showed him lots of things about his family on the internet. He knows you raised his brothers and sisters, but you didn't want him!"

Daci's heart shivered into tiny pieces. "Ah, Paige, you're wrong. I wanted him very much, but I was only a child myself—just ten years old when he was born. I had no say in what happened. I was told he was dead. Do you know where he is?"

At the young woman's nod, tears sprang from Daci's eyes. Jax's arms closed around her, and she collapsed against his chest.

I've found you, Niall. You're alive, and I've found you. Thank You, Jesus!

The tiniest chill closed around her heart. He thought she'd rejected him. Would her little brother welcome her into his life?

* * *

A week later, Jax laid a comforting hand against the small of Daci's back as they stood in the parking lot gazing at the sprawling building of Yeshua House in the same neighborhood of Springfield where she lived. How amazing that he'd been so close to her, and she'd had no knowledge.

Here, her youngest brother had lived all of his twenty-two years. The three-story, redbrick structure, surrounded by neatly trimmed landscaping, displayed flashes of character in the brightly colored shutters framing the many windows and in the ornate porticos that surrounded the three front doorways. The central double doors were emphasized by an extra-wide portico.

"I was afraid the place would look sterile and cold," Daci murmured. "It definitely has an institutional flavor, but with an Ivy League college vibe. This might not be so bad if it's set up homey inside."

"Are you ready to go in?"

She looked up at him, her smile a bit wobbly. "I'm so thankful Niall agreed to see me. But even with seven days to prepare myself mentally and emotionally, I'm still scared stiff."

"It'll be all right. I'll be here for you every

moment. I'm honored you asked me to go on this journey with you."

"I can't think of anyone else I'd rather lean on."

Jax's heart expanded almost too big for his chest, but he consciously dialed down the wattage of his expression to friendly kindness. They hadn't yet had the discussion about a future for them as a couple that he'd intended to start a week ago at her house. The timing hadn't been right.

"What about your siblings?" he said in a teasing tone. "Might be good role reversal to lean on them for a change."

Daci laughed. "Are you kidding? They're as nervous over this as I am. Besides, Niall's counsellor felt that meeting more than one of his siblings at a time might overwhelm him."

"The slow and careful route is best for all, I think."

"Let's do this then." She stepped toward the building, her face resolute.

Inside, the place was indeed set up home-style, with an attractively decorated entry area leading into a large, inviting living room. The reception desk was tucked unobtrusively into the back of the space.

Immediately, a petite, gray-haired woman dressed in work-casual gray slacks and lavender blouse stepped toward them, hand extended. "You must be Candace Marlowe and Jaxton Williams. I'm Mary Blythe, Niall's psychologist and primary counselor. Call me Mary."

"Call me Jax," he said, and shook the offered hand.

"Daci, please." She shook hands in turn.

"Well, Jax and Daci, let's have a little chat before we go see Niall."

She led them up a hall and into a small, neat office and took a seat behind the desk. Jax and Daci settled into padded guest chairs.

The woman's green eyes twinkled at them behind thick glasses. "Niall has been very excited for you to visit, though it's good you agreed to let us have this week to prepare him. We all tend to resist change, but FAS folk are typically less easily adaptable than most."

"We understand." Daci nodded. "If locating him has been an incredible shock for me and my siblings, we can only imagine what it's been like for him—especially since he had the idea we didn't want him."

Mary's gaze went solemn. "On behalf of Yeshua House staff, we apologize for unwittingly fostering that impression. While our Christian values prohibit us from lying, for his sake, while Niall was growing up, we did not volunteer any information to him about his family and hoped he would continue to be content with our love and care. However, he eventually did insist upon specifics a number of years ago, and we shared the minimum information he would allow—his parents' names, the fact that they were dead, etc. Though, of course, we didn't go into the nature of their deaths. When he didn't revisit the conversation, we thought he had forgotten all about it, which is possible for people with his diagnosis, but apparently he and this computer-skilled friend of his have been researching the Marlowe family ever since."

Daci's heart wrenched. "When you had to tell my brother who his family was, wouldn't that have been the time to have contacted me about him?"

Mary sighed. "Unfortunately, our hands were tied as far as initiating contact, though it's a different story now that you have discovered him another way. When he was brought here as an infant, it was among the stipulations tied to the blind trust set up for his care that we do nothing to bring him to the attention of his siblings, especially you."

Daci's nostrils flared. "In other words, my parents paid you to hide him from me."

Mary winced and lowered her gaze.

Jax wound his fingers around the stiff digits of Daci's right hand. "I know you sometimes struggle with anger against your parents over lots of things they did that weren't right or good. But in this case, I believe your mom and dad actually thought this decision through, and tried to do what was best for all of you."

She whipped her head toward him, her gaze fierce. "How can you say that? He was my brother. He—"

"Could they have cared for him?"

"*Would* they have cared for him is the better question, and the answer is no. Caregiving was not in their nature or their character, especially for a child with special needs."

"Exactly. At the age of ten, would *you* have been able to give him the care he needed?"

Daci opened her mouth, but remained mute. Her eyes nearly crossed as she visibly struggled with the answer. Finally, she slumped in her seat. "They could have at least let me know where he was. That he was okay, instead of lying to me that he was dead. I could have stayed in touch with him."

"In that respect, I think the total break was more about your mother's feelings of guilt over Niall's condition."

Daci sniffed. "You may be the only one in the room without a degree in psychology, but

I think you may have nailed that one." She looked toward Mary. "Please accept my apologies. I'm very protective of my siblings."

"Apology accepted. Daci, you remind me of your brother."

"I do?" Her eyes went wide.

"Passionate, selfless, giving. We've been blessed to rear and nurture that young man. The word 'yeshua' is Hebrew for the name Jesus, and it means safety and well-being. This is the foundation we try to provide for our residents as they struggle with both their limitations and their sometimes unusual capabilities."

"Sounds to me like you at Yeshua House have behaved toward him exactly like a family is supposed to do," Jax said. "He's been blessed to be here."

Daci nodded slowly. "I guess I have to say thank you for all you've done for my brother."

Mary laughed. "I'll accept that reluctant gratitude. Hopefully, the feeling will come more naturally after you meet Niall. Follow me."

They went out into the hallway and boarded an elevator.

Mary punched in the number three. "He has chosen to meet his sister in his studio."

"Studio!" Daci stared at the other woman as the elevator climbed.

Jax let out a soft hum. "Unusual capabilities?"

Niall's psychologist adopted a secretive smile, but said nothing further.

They left the elevator, walked up another hallway and stopped in front of a door. The top half was frosted glass, so nothing within could be seen, but an odd whirring sound carried through the barrier.

Beside him, Daci swayed back and forth as her weight shifted one way then the other— the adult version of hopping from foot to foot in nervous anticipation. If it would have been the least bit appropriate for him to hug and reassure her, Jax would have done it, but her attention was anywhere except on him. As it should be.

Mary turned toward him. "Niall wants to meet his sister alone first."

Jax stepped back, and Mary followed suit.

"Go ahead," she urged Daci. "He's expecting you."

Daci's hand gripped the lever-style door latch. Her knuckles were white. She glanced over her shoulder with wild eyes and met Jax's gaze.

"God is in this," he said softly.

Slowly, her whole being visibly relaxed, and she smiled. "Yes, He is."

Daci opened the door and went inside. Jax's heart went with her.

Three hours later, Daci stood with Jax on the porch outside her apartment, still unable to contain the excitement that bubbled within her like fizz in a shaken can of soda. Spontaneously, she threw her arms around Jax.

"He's amazing!"

"So you've been telling me." His chuckle rumbled in her ear pressed to his chest.

Cheeks heating, Daci pulled away from him. He must think she was a complete nut, babbling nonstop about her visit with Niall and now hugging him out of the blue.

His hand came up and cupped her cheek while his thumb traced her cheekbone. Her heart nearly tripped over itself.

A tender smile lit his face. "How often does a person find out their long-lost brother is an award-winning potter? I'm so happy for you."

"I can hardly believe it." She held up a gracefully curved vase glazed with elegant swirls of gold and blue. "As soon as he was told I wanted him after all, my sweet, forgiving baby brother got busy and made this for me. He does the glaze and everything, but not the firing. For safety's sake, the art supervisor does that. I mean, Niall struggles to write his name, but those same hands form something like this on a potter's wheel. How can that be? I'm just…just…"

"Amazed?" Jax's gaze was teasing.

"Right." She laughed. "Sure, he has some of the distinctive FAS facial features, but he also looks like a family member with our particular shade of brown eyes and stubborn chin."

"I'd call it a determined chin. Very attractive, by the way. Like the rest of you."

Daci gaped up at him. Did he genuinely find her attractive?

His lips curved in a wry smile. "Candace Marlowe, you are one of the smartest, most discerning women I know, but I see I'm going to have to spell out for you what I've been trying to say for a while now."

His arms tugged her close, and she gazed into his crystal-blue eyes, speechless.

"I'm crazy about you," he continued. "In the past five years, you're the only woman who has made me want to love again. You could be a trapeze artist without a net for all that the risks of your career matter to me anymore. I'm done protecting my heart in a cage of my own making. The only question is, how do you feel about me?"

With a soft sob, Daci buried her nose in the lapel of his polo shirt. His wood-spice scent failed to dizzy her head half as thoroughly as his declaration had done. She lifted her face to his.

"I think this day just went from wonderful to perfect. Jaxton Williams, you're in for more trouble than you can handle, because I'm never letting you go."

"Bring it on," he murmured as his warm lips found hers.

* * * * *

If you enjoyed this story, don't miss these other action-packed adventures from Jill Elizabeth Nelson:

FRAME-UP
SHAKE DOWN
ROCKY MOUNTAIN SABOTAGE

Find more great reads at
www.LoveInspired.com.

Dear Reader,

With drug-and-alcohol addiction a widespread problem throughout the world, it is dismaying the number of children profoundly impacted from birth and throughout their lives by the substance abuse of their parents. FASD (Fetal Alcohol Spectrum Disorder) is a type of birth disability traced directly to the mother's consumption of alcohol during pregnancy. The amount consumed does not need to be frequent, regular or in large amounts in order to affect the infant developing in the womb.

FAS children do not always have the outward characteristics described in this novel and may appear physically normal, though their brains are deeply affected. While many birth disabilities are genetic in nature, FASD is 100 percent preventable and dependent on the parents' wise choices to abstain from alcohol consumption during pregnancy.

In 2016, the Centers for Disease Control and Prevention released a fact sheet estimating that one out of twenty school-age children may be suffering from some level of FASD. Unfortunately, the number may be much higher, because alcohol-related disabilities are often misdiagnosed or undiagnosed. The National

Organization on Fetal Alcohol Syndrome is working to raise awareness among health-care providers and the public. For more information, including symptoms to look for in a child, go to www.nofas.org.

I hope Daci's story has given you cause to think outside the box about socioeconomic status and substance abuse related to child neglect and endangerment. Wealth did little to help Daci in her growing-up years, and poverty did not stop Serena from passionately seeking whatever help she needed to change her behaviors and raise her own child.

For more information on other books I've written, to sign up for my newsletter, or send me a note, drop by jillelizabethnelson.com. I'd love to hear from you!

Abundant Blessings,
Jill

Get 2 Free Books,
<u>Plus</u> 2 Free Gifts—
just for trying the Reader Service!

Love Inspired

YES! Please send me 2 FREE Love Inspired® Romance novels and my 2 FREE mystery gifts (gifts are worth about $10 retail). After receiving them, if I don't wish to receive any more books, I can return the shipping statement marked "cancel." If I don't cancel, I will receive 6 brand-new novels every month and be billed just $5.24 for the regular-print edition or $5.74 each for the larger-print edition in the U.S., or $5.74 each for the regular-print edition or $6.24 each for the larger-print edition in Canada. That's a saving of at least 13% off the cover price. It's quite a bargain! Shipping and handling is just 50¢ per book in the U.S. and 75¢ per book in Canada.* I understand that accepting the 2 free books and gifts places me under no obligation to buy anything. I can always return a shipment and cancel at any time. The free books and gifts are mine to keep no matter what I decide.

Please check one:
- ☐ Love Inspired Romance Regular-Print
  (105/305 IDN GMWU)
- ☐ Love Inspired Romance Larger-Print
  (122/322 IDN GMWU)

Name	(PLEASE PRINT)

Address	Apt. #

City	State/Province	Zip/Postal Code

Signature (if under 18, a parent or guardian must sign)

Mail to the **Reader Service:**
IN U.S.A.: P.O. Box 1341, Buffalo, NY 14240-8531
IN CANADA: P.O. Box 603, Fort Erie, Ontario L2A 5X3

Want to try two free books from another line?
Call 1-800-873-8635 today or visit www.ReaderService.com.

*Terms and prices subject to change without notice. Prices do not include applicable taxes. Sales tax applicable in N.Y. Canadian residents will be charged applicable taxes. Offer not valid in Quebec. This offer is limited to one order per household. Books received may not be as shown. Not valid for current subscribers to Love Inspired Romance books. All orders subject to approval. Credit or debit balances in a customer's account(s) may be offset by any other outstanding balance owed by or to the customer. Please allow 4 to 6 weeks for delivery. Offer available while quantities last.

Your Privacy—The Reader Service is committed to protecting your privacy. Our Privacy Policy is available online at www.ReaderService.com or upon request from the Reader Service.

We make a portion of our mailing list available to reputable third parties that offer products we believe may interest you. If you prefer that we not exchange your name with third parties, or if you wish to clarify or modify your communication preferences, please visit us at www.ReaderService.com/consumerschoice or write to us at Reader Service Preference Service, P.O. Box 9062, Buffalo, NY 14240-9062. Include your complete name and address.

LII7R3

HOMETOWN HEARTS ♥

YES! Please send me **The Hometown Hearts Collection** in Larger Print. This collection begins with 3 FREE books and 2 FREE gifts in the first shipment. Along with my 3 free books, I'll also get the next 4 books from the Hometown Hearts Collection, in LARGER PRINT, which I may either return and owe nothing, or keep for the low price of $4.99 U.S./ $5.89 CDN each plus $2.99 for shipping and handling per shipment*. If I decide to continue, about once a month for 8 months I will get 6 or 7 more books, but will only need to pay for 4. That means 2 or 3 books in every shipment will be FREE! If I decide to keep the entire collection, I'll have paid for only 32 books because 19 books are FREE! I understand that accepting the 3 free books and gifts places me under no obligation to buy anything. I can always return a shipment and cancel at any time. My free books and gifts are mine to keep no matter what I decide.

262 HCN 3432 462 HCN 3432

Name	(PLEASE PRINT)

Address	Apt. #

City	State/Prov.	Zip/Postal Code

Signature (if under 18, a parent or guardian must sign)

Mail to the **Reader Service:**
IN U.S.A.: P.O. Box 1867, Buffalo, NY. 14240-1867
IN CANADA: P.O. Box 609, Fort Erie, Ontario L2A 5X3

* Terms and prices subject to change without notice. Prices do not include applicable taxes. Sales tax applicable in NY. Canadian residents will be charged applicable taxes. This offer is limited to one order per household. All orders subject to approval. Credit or debit balances in a customer's account(s) may be offset by any other outstanding balance owed by or to the customer. Please allow 4 to 6 weeks for delivery. Offer available while quantities last. Offer not available to Quebec residents.

Your Privacy—The Reader Service is committed to protecting your privacy. Our Privacy Policy is available online at www.ReaderService.com or upon request from the Reader Service.

We make a portion of our mailing list available to reputable third parties that offer products we believe may interest you. If you prefer that we not exchange your name with third parties, or if you wish to clarify or modify your communication preferences, please visit us at www.ReaderService.com/consumerschoice or write to us at Reader Service Preference Service, P.O. Box 9062, Buffalo, NY. 14240-9062. Include your complete name and address.